THE MOST PLEASANT
HISTORY OF
Tom a Lincolne

R I

Printed by J. W. for B. Deacon at the Angel in Gilt-spur-street. 1704.

T A L

R.I.,
THE MOST
PLEASANT HISTORY
OF
Tom a Lincolne

EDITED BY

RICHARD S. M. HIRSCH

Published for THE NEWBERRY LIBRARY
by the UNIVERSITY OF SOUTH CAROLINA PRESS
Columbia, South Carolina

Library of Congress Cataloging in Publication Data

Johnson, Richard, 1573?–1659?
    The most pleasant history of Tom a Lincolne.
    (Publications of the Renaissance English
Text Society ; v. 7–8)
    Bibliography: p.
    1. Arthurian romances. I. J., R.
II. R. J. III. Hirsch, Richard S. M., 1945–
IV. Title. V. Series: Renaissance English
Text Society. Publications ; v. 7–8.
PR2296.J6M6   1978   823'.4   78–14405
ISBN 0–87249–358–X

FOR

Sears and Mae Jayne

Table of Contents

Acknowledgments

N THE COURSE OF PREPARING THIS edition I have been helped and encouraged by more people than it is possible to name here. The copy-text and facsimile of the two title pages are reprinted by permission of the Folger Shakespeare Library, Washington, D.C., for whose generosity I am grateful. I wish also to thank the Library of Worcester College, Oxford, (and particularly the late Dr. R. A. Sayce), for providing reproductions of other texts and permission to collate them; the Syndics of the Cambridge University Library, for permission to reproduce the woodcut used as a frontispiece in this edition from a copy of the 1704 printing of *Tom a Lincolne* in their possession; the Rare Book staffs of the Rockefeller Library, Brown University, and the Cambridge University Library (particularly Mr. J. C. T. Oates, F. B. A., Deputy Librarian), for much help and indulgence over the years; Miss Katherine F. Pantzer of the Houghton Library, Harvard, for vital information speedily delivered; Professors Leicester Bradner and James G. McManaway, for examining certain manuscript alterations in the copy-text; and Professors George K. Anderson, Andrew J. Sabol, Robert Scholes, and Stuart C. Sherman, all of Brown University, for much help and good advice in the early stages of this project. In the difficult work of reading the proofs of the text against the copy-text I was greatly helped by my friend L. M. Shushansky, and by my father, Milton Hirsch, who each contributed hours of patient and accurate labor. My colleagues Professors Joseph H. Harkey, L. Anderson Orr, and Roland Q. Nicholson read the proofs of the Introduction and Notes. My friend Dean Reed helped in verifying the line-numbers

and the explanatory and textual note numbers keyed to them, and also checked through the corrected proofs of the Introduction.

Special thanks are due to Professors G. Blakemore Evans, Richard S. Sylvester and David M. Bevington, past and present officers of The Renaissance English Text Society, for many helpful suggestions.

All of these generous people have helped me to correct numerous errors and to avoid others into which I would otherwise have fallen. Any errors which remain are of course my own.

My greatest debt, and a continuing one, is to Professor Sears Jayne, to whom, with his lovely wife, this edition is most affectionately dedicated.

Introduction

T FIRST GLANCE, *The Most Pleasant History of Tom a Lincolne* seems a rather conventional Renaissance prose romance. It is Arthurian, if only nominally so; it retains the neutral moral tone of the medieval romances from which it descends; it episodically exhausts a large supply of dragons, villains, and ladies-in-distress; and it is divided into two parts, apparently for the usual commercial reasons.[1]

Closer examination, however, reveals that its conventionality is largely superficial. For example, so far from being any recognizable version of the great Tudor myth of Arthur as the sum of all the chivalric virtues, a myth which found its purest expression in *The Faerie Queene*,[2] the Arthur of *Tom a Lincolne* is an adulterer, a sacrilegist, and a very poor judge of human nature, who not surprisingly ends by wrecking his kingdom.

Again, though the division into two parts may have been primarily commercial in origin, something else must have been at work as well, since the two parts seem to have very different literary aims. Part I, which

---

[1] Romances and other works of popular literature were often published in parts, perhaps for the reasons that Anthony Munday, author and translator of many of these, alleges: that "a Booke growing too bigge in quantitie, is Profitable neither to the minde nor the purse: for . . . the first Part will entice them to haue the second, [and] . . . a man grutched not so much at a little money, payd at seuerall times, as hee doth at once." (From *Palmerin D'Oliua. The First Part* [edition of 1637], "To the Reader." Quoted in Louis B. Wright, *Middle-Class Culture in Elizabethan England* (Ithaca, N. Y., 1958), p. 380.

[2] For the background of this myth see Florence Brinkley, *Arthurian Legend in the Seventeenth Century* (Baltimore, 1932).

seems intended mainly to entertain the reader, recounts the adultery of Arthur and the resulting birth of Tom at Lincoln, his upbringing, adventures, and his own sexual entanglements, which include fathering a bastard, abandoning the mother, and contracting marriage with someone else, all of which is narrated in a strictly neutral moral tone. But in Part II, though the tone remains neutral, the aim is clearly to instruct as well as entertain, since the reader soon discovers that the adventures in Part I do have moral consequences.

Tom had deserted his presumed parents, and later abandoned his pregnant mistress; in Part II he is himself deserted by his wife and their son, and, when he follows them, is murdered by the wife and her new lover. Arthur's queen (who bears no resemblance to Guinevere) after Arthur's death murders his mistress, Tom's mother, and ends a suicide; Tom's wife (or widow, she having murdered him) is in turn murdered by their son in a revenge motif reminiscent of the *Oresteia*.

One soon realizes that despite the misleadingly neutral moral tone and the tradition of moral neutrality which the author had inherited from medieval romance, *Tom a Lincolne* is, as it stands, essentially a moral work, whether or not it was a moral aim which underlay the division into two parts.

At least two possibilities suggest themselves as reasons for this added moral dimension of the second part. Either the author, perhaps having received criticism from friends (or enemies) suggesting that the conduct of his characters had been too licentious in Part I, decided to "put the snaffle in their mouths," as Ben Jonson says in the Dedication of *Volpone* that he had done to them that cry out "We never punish vice . . . ;" or, as the last paragraph of Part I suggests, the author already had at least the broad outline of Part II in mind (perhaps had already written it), and had early on decided, like Ascham in *The Scholemaster* and Starkey in *England in Henry VIII's Time*, among other Renaissance writers, to organize his matter into two parts, in this case showing heroic exploits in Part I, and moral retribution for them in Part II.

In any case, whether or not it was intentionally aimed, the effect on the reader must have been similar to what Stanley Fish sees Milton accomplishing in his portrait of Satan in *Paradise Lost:*[3] the reader first admires and wishes to emulate the hero, and then, seeing the hero justly punished for his misdeeds, himself feels guilty for having admired him, and is brought to a new sense of what is truly admirable. This would be a valuable attraction for a work to boast at a time when, as Louis B. Wright points out, "Feeling the stab of his conscience whenever he succumbed to the allurements of mere amusement, [the reader] wanted to believe that there was mingled in his literary entertainment both profit and instruction."[4]

Commercial success may have been a primary motive for moralizing, but, once entered, moralism has attractions of its own, and the breadth and subtlety of the moral view of the book suggest, to me at least, that the theme of the work is more deeply moral than it needed to be merely for popular success.

A number of critics discuss *Tom a Lincolne* briefly in passing,[5] usually to condemn it as un-Arthurian or immoral (or overly moral), and it seems never to have been considered a serious attempt at moral fiction. The relationship between the moral stance and the two-part structure has not previously been noted.

The sources of *Tom a Lincolne* were probably as numerous as the works that the author knew, but only a few specific probable sources can be mentioned here. The names of the three knights, Lancelot, Tristram and Triamore, who are singled out in Part I, seem to come from Christopher Middleton's *Chinon of England* (1597),[6] where the same three knights (and only they) appear. The Blacke Knight's interview with

[3] *Surpriz'd by Sin: The Reader in Paradise Lost* (New York, 1967), passim.
[4] Wright, p. 100.
[5] E. A. Baker, *The History of the British Novel* (London, 1924–39), II, 197; Florence Brinkley (see note 2 above), p. 97; R. W. Barber, *Arthur of Albion* (New York, 1961), p. 138; Mary Patchell, *The Palmerin Romances in Elizabethan Prose Fiction* (New York, 1947), p. 107; Walter R. Davis, *Idea and Act in Elizabethan Fiction* (Princeton, 1969), pp. 226–7 (the best reading of the work); John O'Connor, *Amadis de Gaule and its Influence on Elizabethan Literature* (New Brunswick, N.J., 1970), p. 205; and James D. Merriman, *The Flower of Kings: Arthurian Legend in England, 1485–1835* (Lawrence, Kansas, 1973), p. 48.
[6] Ed. W. E. Mead, E.E.T.S. Orig. Ser. CLXV (1925).

xiii

his murdered father's ghost in Part II so closely parallels Hamlet's interview with his father's ghost (*Hamlet* I.v.9–25), that it seems almost certainly to have been derived from it.[7] The story of Angellica, Arthur's mistress who is shut up in a nunnery and eventually murdered by Arthur's jealous wife, seems likely to derive from the legend of Rosamond, mistress of Henry II, who had a similar fate, and whose story was available in a number of forms at the time *Tom a Lincolne* appeared.[8] The hero's name almost certainly comes from the famous bell of Lincoln Cathedral, which was called Tom (a favorite English name for bells and foundlings) long before *Tom a Lincolne* was seen in print.[9] The titles of the Red-rose Knight, the Palmer, and the Queen of the Fayrieland may ultimately be Spenserian in origin.

The style of *Tom a Lincolne* is, like its plot, and many of the incidents, indebted to other contemporary works of prose fiction. Thus we find that, like Deloney in *Jacke of Newburie* (1597 and 1598) and Lodge in *Rosalind* (1590), the author employs both a plain and an ornamented style, varying their use according to the necessities of his narrative. His plain style he uses generally to begin a new chapter, to narrate

[7] D. A. Robertson, Jr., "Richard Johnson and *The Seven Champions of Christendome*, 1596 and 1597," unpub. diss. (Princeton, 1940), p. 87. I am inclined to believe that *Tom a Lincolne* is indebted to *Hamlet* not only for the interview between son and ghost, but also for the idea of Anglitora's adultery and murder of Tom, which is the chief narrative structure of Part II. For a discussion of this and the other probable sources of *Tom a Lincolne*, see my dissertation, "A Critical Edition of Richard Johnson's *Tom a Lincolne*" (Brown, 1972), pp. 76–77, and Ch. 3 passim.

[8] The chief works dealing with Rosamond in the period are: William Warner's *Albion's England* (London, G. Robinson, 1586; STC 25079), Ch. XLI; "A Mournefull Dittie, on the Death of Rosamond, King Henry the second's Concubine," in Thomas Deloney, *The Garland of Good Will* (ent. in SR 5 March 1593); Samuel Daniel, "The Complaint of Rosamond," in *Delia* (London, J. C[harlwood], 1592; STC 6253); Michael Drayton, *England's Heroical Epistles* (London, J. R[oberts], 1597; STC 7193); and the anonymous comedy *Looke About You* (London, for W. Ferbrand, 1600; STC 16799). For a discussion of the Rosamond material in connection with *Tom a Lincolne*, see my dissertation, pp. 78–79.

[9] "Thou shouldst heare Tom a Lincolne roare." comments Thomas Nashe in *Foure Letters Confuted* (London, 1592) ed. R. B. McKerrow, *The Works of Thomas Nashe* (London, 1904), I, 321; as quoted in Robertson, p. 81.

simple events, and to effect a transition from one locale to another, especially at the ends of chapters. Three examples of this sort are given below:

1. (Beginning of Chap. VI.)

The next Morning by the breake of day, the Red-rose Knight rose from his Cabbin, and went vpon the Hatches of the Shippe, casting his eyes round about, to see if hee could espie some Towne or Cittie where they might take harbour: and in looking about hee espied a great spacious Cittie, in the middle whereof stood a most sumptuous Pallace, hauing many high Towers standing in the ayre like the Grecian Piramides, the which he supposed to be the Pallace of some great Potentate: therefore calling Sir Lancelot (with two other Knights) vnto him, hee requested them to goe vp into the Citie, and to enquire of the Countrey, and who was the Gouernour thereof; . . .

2. (Part II, Chap. IV.)

The Knight of the Castle hearing this, came downe and met them in a large square Court paued with marble stone, where hee kindly gaue them entertainement, promising them both lodging and other needfull things they were destitute of.

The three Trauellers accepted of his courtesies, and being long before weather-beaten on the Seas, thought themselues from a deepe dungeon of calamities lifted to the toppe of all pleasures and prosperitie; . . .

3. (Part II, Chap. III.)

Heere will wee leaue the dead to their quiet restes, and returne to the Blacke Knight, and his Mother Anglitora, with the Indian slaue that attends them: for strange bee the accidents that happen to them in forraigne Countryes: and after, wee will speake what hapned to the Red-rose Knight on the Sea.

As one can see, although the sentences are sometimes very long (the first example goes on for another eleven lines before it ends), they are extremely simple. In example No. 1 above, the author has written three perfectly good, perhaps even graceful, sentences, but perhaps fearing that they were too short and unsophisticated, has strung them together with an *and* and a *therefore*. One will note also in example No. 1 the phrase "standing in the ayre like the Grecian Piramides," which shows us both his favorite simple rhetorical figure, *similitudo* (simile), and a (not entirely accurate) classical allusion. The diction is always plain; except for a few words which have passed out of the language, a child would find little problem with the author's vocabulary. The tone of his narrative is one of complete control over the narrative process. It is the professional story-teller's tone, which says "Just sit back and listen: I will take care of everything." Because of the professional quality of the narrative tone there is no sense at any time of the real personality behind the story-teller's voice, and just as there is, as mentioned above, no intrusive commentary on events, there is also no sense of irony. Before leaving the discussion of his plain style, let us note that here the author occasionally uses simple rhetorical figures, as in example No. 2, where, near the end of the passage, he ornaments his expression with *translatio*, or metaphor ("dungeon of calamitie"); *restrictio* ("from . . . to"); and *alliteratio* ("deepe dungeon," "pleasures and prosperitie").

The author's ornamented style, of which three examples are given below, is used in all the conventional places: in descriptions, either of places or objects (including people), in passages which attempt to describe the emotions which a character is experiencing, and, of course, in set-speeches.

1. (Chap. I.)

Amongst these glorious troupes of London Ladyes, Angellica the Earles daughter had the chiefest prayse for beauty and courtly behauiour: for euen as the siluer-shining Moone in a Winters frosty night, surpasseth the brightest of the twinckling Stars: so farre Angellicaes sweete feature exceeded the rest of the Ladyes: whereby King Arthur was so intangled in the snares of loue, that by no meanes he could withdraw his affections from her diuine excellence. He that before delighted to tread a weary march after Bellonas Drummes, was now constrayned to trace Cupids Measures in Ladyes Chambers: and could as well straine the strings of a Lovers Lute, as sound a Souldiers alarme in the field:

2. (Chap. I.)

By this time, the golden Sunne began to glister on the Mountaine top, and his sister Luna to withdraw her waterish countenance: at which time, the pleasant Shepheards began to tune their Morning notes, and to repayre vnto their foulded Sheepe, according to their woonted manner: Amongst which crue of lusty Swaines, old Antonio approached foorth of his Gate with a chearefull countenance, whose Beard was as white as polished Siluer, or like to Snow lying vpon the Northerne Mountaines:

3.   (Chap. V.)

Man of all other creatures (most vertuous Lady) is most miserable, for Nature hath ordayned to euery Bird a pleasant tune to bemoane their misshapps, the Nightingale doth complaine her Rape and lost Virginitie within the desart Groues: the Swanne doth likewise sing a dolefull heauie tune a while before shee dyes, as though Heauen had inspired her with some foreknowledge of things to come. You Madame, now must sing your Swan-like Song; for the pretty Birds (I see) doe drope their hanging heads and mourne, to thinke that you must die. Maruell not Madame; the angry Queene will haue it so. Accurst am I in being constrayned to bee the bloody instrument of so tyrannous a fact. Accurst am I that haue ordained that cuppe, which must by Poyson, stanche the thirst of the bloody Empresse: and most accursed am I, that cannot withstand the angry Fates, which haue appoynted mee to offer outrage vnto vertue.

Here we see the author using many more of the rhetorical devices at his command in the attempt to raise his style to the level of the important and dramatic events which he is narrating. The three passages chosen, the description of Angellica and of her effect on Arthur, the description of Antonio (given just prior to the finding of Tom), and the speech of the Doctor at the moment of his supposed murder of Dulcippa (in Lancelot's narrative), demonstrate how much more carefully than in his plain style the author could write. Thus, his sentences, which in the plain style are rambling, here are balanced and precise. One of his few attempts at Euphuism, the passage in example No. 1, shows that he could carry it off quite well. He has carefully planned not only the properly Euphuistic parts of the passage (the balanced *parison* in lines 4, 5, 6, 7, and 10, 11, 12, 13 and 14), but also the opening sentence, which is almost pure iambic pentameter, and the sound of the passage throughout, relying as much on assonance as on alliteration, and thus avoiding some of the more unfortunate Euphuistic effects. Example No. 2 furnishes us proof that the author was not one to borrow from one literary fashion at the expense of another, for just as he imitated Euphuism in Example 1, he echoes, if he does not quite manage to recreate, Arcadianism in the second. Even if we were not to notice *prosopopoeia* (personification of natural phenomena) in line 2, the "pleasant Shepheards" tuning their "Morning notes" and the whole evocation of the conventional pastoral setting, including the name Antonio—what English midlands shepherd ever had so obviously Italian a name?—would convince us that he is here borrowing from the tradition which Sidney's great work exemplifies. In Example No. 3 the author without imitating any one literary fashion very closely, has constructed a brief oration, effective for the Doctor, a sympathetic and dignified character, to speak at his last interview with Dulcippa. It opens with the conventional *sententia*, the use of a general remark (on birds, in this case) which is first shored up with *exempla* (the Nightingale and Swan), and then applied to the case at hand, the death of Dulcippa. This exposition, which, though emotional, is also restrained, intending to introduce the subject of Dulcippa's death as gently and sympathetically as possible, is, in a sense, also a brief dramatic monologue, since in the phrase "Maruell not Madame" the Doctor is responding to some action or expression of Dulcippa's which is not otherwise indicated. It is partly this response which the Doctor sees, but which we do not, that leads him from the restrained tone of his exposition to *lamentatio* in lamenting his fate as murderer which follows immediately. The *anaphora* and *incrementum* used in this lament tremendously add to its final emotional power. The author knew where to stop, for the abrupt end of the Doctor's speech is far more dramatic than any continuation would have been.

This discussion of the author's style in *Tom a Lincolne*, while it has made no attempt to mention every device which he uses, should show the reader that though he may not have been a highly skilled or original stylist, he was at least a conscious one.

Thus, although many of the incidents and much of the style are imitative of earlier literature, the author, partly by means of the moral stance and the two-part structure, and partly by making his imitation generally judicious, produces from this varied stock an original and interesting synthesis of his own.[10]

Authorship, Date, Printing History

Tom a Lincolne is generally accepted as the work of Richard Johnson (1573?–1659?), whose initials follow the dedication. Johnson mentions the character Tom a Lincolne in the preface to his *The History of Tom Thvmbe* (1621),[11] and the unique copy of the earliest edition of *Tom a Lincolne* (1631) carries the manuscript attribution "Richard Johnson" on the dedication-page, in what may be the hand of William Cole (1714–82), the first recorded owner.

Part I of *Tom a Lincolne* is first heard of as having been entered in the Stationers' Register to W. White "by assignment from Wydowe Danter" on 24 December 1599 (Arber, III, 153), though no earlier entry of the work to Danter or his widow has been found. Since no earlier entry seems to exist, and there is no other evidence of earlier printings, it seems reasonable to assume that Johnson wrote Part I of *Tom a Lincolne* in the interval between the publication of his *The Seauen Champions of Christendome* (in two parts, 1596 and 1597) and the date upon which Part I of *Tom a Lincolne* was entered in 1599.

Part II of *Tom a Lincolne* was entered on 20 October 1607 (Arber, III, 362), and is unlikely to have been written earlier than 1600–1601, since one of its probable sources, Shakespeare's *Hamlet*, from which the Blacke Knight's interview with his angry father's ghost almost certainly derives, was first produced that season.

Though Part I was complete by 1599 and Part II by 1607, no edition of either part is known to exist before the sixth edition, printed by

[10] For a fuller discussion of the style of the work, see my dissertation, pp. 105–11.

[11] (London, for Thomas Langley) *STC* 14056. The unique copy is now in the Pierpont Morgan Library; ed. C. F. Bühler (Evanston, Ill., Northwestern University Press for the Renaissance English Text Society, 1965).

Augustine Mathewes for R. Byrde and F. Coules in 1631 (*STC* 14684). Since the edition marked the sixth is dated 1631, a long time after 1599–1607, and this is a popular sort of work, likely to go through many editions, there is no reason not to believe that the first five editions once existed, though they have left no trace.

The work seems to have continued popular after 1631 as well, since new editions appeared in 1635 (7th; A. M. for F. Faulkner and F. Coules; *STC* 14685); 1655 (9th; T. R. and E. M. for Francis Coles; Wing J807); 1668 (G. Purslowe for F. Coles; Wing J810); and apparently two in 1682 (12th [and 13th?]; H. Brugis for W. Thackeray; Wing J808 and J809); as well as another edition, called the thirteenth, by J. W. for B. Deacon, in 1704.

Richard Johnson, Freeman of London

Of the life of Richard Johnson (1573?–1659?), almost nothing is known with certainty, not even the dates of his birth and death.[12] He seems first to have been an apprentice, and later a freeman of London,[13] though of what company is not known. His career as a writer spanned the thirty years between 1591 and 1621, and in that time he produced a number of elegies, many ballads, two public-spirited pamphlets, a jest book, an antiquarian tract, a version of the Tom Thumb story, and two very popular prose romances, *The Seauen Champions of Christendome*, his best-known work (printed 1596–7), and *Tom a Lincolne*, the work here edited. At least two of his works, *Anglorum Lacrimae* (1603) and *Look on Me London* (1613), were very largely borrowed from the

[12] Both the dates 1573 and 1659 were announced without supporting authority by the eminent scholar and forger J. P. Collier, *A Bibliographical and Critical Account of the Rarest Books in the English Language* (London, 1865), II, 183. Since Collier cited no authority, and is known to have been fond of fabricating, there is no good reason to accept them.

[13] Johnson mentions in the dedication to *The Nine Worthies of London* (1592) that he is "a poore apprentice," and signed many of his later works (including *The Pleasant Walkes of Moore-fields*, *The Pleasant Conceites of Old Hobson, the Merry Londoner*, both 1607; and *Look on Me London*, 1613) as a "freeman of this Citty."

published works of other writers,[14] though this seems to have gone unnoticed until our own time.

Though Johnson undoubtedly lived in London throughout his writing career, he may possibly have been born in Huntingdonshire, since he dedicates *Tom a Lincolne* to one "Simon Wortedge of Okenberrie (Alconbury) in the County of Huntington," in terms which suggest that their parents were well acquainted, and signs the dedication "Your worships . . . Countreyman, R. I."

A list of Johnson's known writings follows; the number in parentheses at the end of each entry indicates the number of known or probable editions through 1700.

[1591] *Musarum Plangores* (Not in *STC*) (1)

1592 *The Nine Worthies of London* (*STC* 14686) (2)

1596–7 *The Seauen Champions of Christendome* (*STC* 14677–8) (14)

1599–1607 *The Most Pleasant History of Tom a Lincolne* (6th ed., *STC* 14684) (12)

1603 *Anglorum Lacrimae* (Not in *STC*) (1)

1603 *A Lanterne-light for Loyall Subiects* (*STC* 14675) (1)

1607 *The Pleasant Walkes of Moore-fields* (*STC* 14690) (1)

1607 *The Pleasant Conceites of Old Hobson, the Merry Londoner* (*STC* 14688) (4)

1612 *A Crowne Garland of Goulden Roses* (*STC* 14672) (7)

1612 *A Remembrance of the Honours Due . . . To Robert Earle of Salisbury* (*STC* 14691) (1)

1613 *Look on Me London* (*STC* 14676) (1)

1620? *The Golden Garland of Princely Pleasures* (*STC* 14674 "Third Impression") (13)

1621 *The History of Tom Thvmbe* (*STC* 14056) (1)

The more important studies of Johnson are the following:

Bryant, J. H. "Richard Johnson's *Musarum Plangores.*" *Renaissance Notes* XVI (1963): 94–98.

---

[14] See Franklin B. Williams, Jr., "Richard Johnson's Borrowed Tears," *SP*, XXXIV:2 (April 1937), 186–90; and Richard S. M. Hirsch, "The Source of Richard Johnson's *Look on Me London*," *English Language Notes* XIII, 2 (December 1975), 107–13.

Bühler, C. F. Introduction to ed. *The History of Tom Thvmbe*. Evanston, Ill.: Northwestern University Press for the Renaissance English Text Society, 1965.

Chester, A. G. "Richard Johnson's *Golden Garland.*" *Modern Language Quarterly* X (March 1949): 61–7.

Hirsch, R. S. M. "A Critical Edition of Richard Johnson's *Tom a Lincolne.*" Unpublished dissertation: Brown, 1972.

————. "The Source of Richard Johnson's *Look on Me London.*" *English Language Notes*, XIII, 2 (December 1975), 107–13.

Robertson, D. A., Jr. "Richard Johnson and *The Seven Champions of Christendome.*" Unpublished dissertation: Princeton, 1940.

Williams, F. B., Jr. "Richard Johnson's Borrowed Tears." *Studies in Philology* XXXIV (April 1937): 186–90.

Willkomm, H. W. *Über Richard Johnson's Seven Champions of Christendom*. Berlin, 1911.

THE TEXT: Description of Sources

Tom a Lincolne exists in a number of early printings; the three earliest have been collated for this edition.

1631. [Within a border of type ornaments] The most pleasant History § of TOM § A LINCOLNE, § That renowned Souldier, the § RED-ROSE Knight, who for § his Valour and Chivalry, was surna- § med *The Boast of England.* § Shewing his Honourable Victories in Forraigne § Countries, with his strange Fortunes in the *Fayrie* § Land: and how he married the faire *Anglitora,* § Daughter to *Prester Iohn,* that re-nowned § Monarke of the World. § Together with the Lives aud [*sic*] Deathes of his two § famous Sonnes, the *Blacke Knight,* and the *Fayrie* § *Knight,* with divers other memorable ac- § cidents, full of delight. § *The sixth Impression* § [rule] § *LONDON,* § Printed by *Aug: Mathewes* and are to bee sold by § *Robert Byrde,* and *Francis Coules.* 1631. § *STC* 14684.

Quarto in 4s: A-M⁴N². [A1] blank, as are A2ᵛ, A3ᵛ, H2ᵛ, H3ᵛ, and

N2^v. [A2] title; A3 dedication; A4 (missigned A3)-H^v text of Part One unpaged; H2 title to Part Two: THE § Second Part of the § Famous Historie of Tom a Lin- § colne, the Red-rose Knight. § *Wherein is declared his vnfortunate* § Death, his Ladyes disloyalty, his Chil- § drens Honours, and lastly, his Death § most strangely reuenged. § [rule] § *Written by the first Author.* § [rule] § [printer's device, Mc-Kerrow 379] § At London printed by *Augustine Matthewes*, § dwelling in the Parsonage House of *Saint* § *Brides* in Fleete-street. 1631.; H3 To the Reader; H4–N2 text of Part Two unpaged.

The running title, "Tom a Lincolne § the Red-rose Knight." is replaced on H^r by the headline *"The bloody Letter of Queene* Caelia," since there was not room on the page for both the headline and the recto half of the running title. The variant verso headline "Tom a Lincolne." occurs on B3^v, B4^v, C^v, C2^v, D2^v, D3^v, E3^v, E4^v, F^v, F2^v, G^v, G4^v, H^v, I3^v, I4^v, K3^v, K4^v, L3^v, L4^v, M3^v, and M4^v.

Three errors were made in printing the catchwords: on G the catch-word of F4^v, "soone", is omitted from the text; on G4^v the catchword of G4, "it", is omitted from the text; and on K4 the catchword, "drown-ing", is misspelled "drownig". The text is printed in black letter, 38 lines to the page.

The Folger Shakespeare Library copy, the only one known to exist, measures 14.0 × 18.5 cm., and is bound in late-eighteenth-century brown leather. Aside from what appears to be an early pressmark in brown ink, on the title page, there are five manuscript additions or alterations in the volume. The first, on A3, is the addition, also in brown ink, of the name "Richard Johnson" just below the initials R. I. at the end of the dedication. The second, on C2, is the alteration (and oblitera-tion) of a word ("Turkish" in the 7th ed.) by the word "Spanish" written over it. The third, on C2^v, is the substitution of the word "sail-ing" for the word "trauell", the latter being only partly obscured. The fourth, on D^v, is the substitution of the word "Dieties" [sic] for a word ("God" in the 7th ed.) which is rendered illegible, if not invisible. The fifth and last, on L3, is the complete obliteration of a parenthetical phrase ("as did the blood of Abell" in the 7th ed.) without anything being substituted for it. These last four alterations are in black ink.

Professors Leicester Bradner and James G. McManaway, who have been kind enough to examine these alterations for me, conclude that while they are too brief to be positive about, they seem to date from the seventeenth or eighteenth century. The first two, in brown ink, are clearly a pressmark and an attribution, respectively. The source of the four "emendations" in the text itself, which are in black ink and in another hand, is probably some opinionated early owner of the volume who wanted its politics, geography, and theological usage to agree with his own.

The provenance of the copy is as follows: William Cole (1714–1782); Britwell Court; Sir R. Leicester Harmsworth; Folger Shakespeare Library. Sig. A2^v bears the William Cole bookplate, while the Harmsworth and Folger Library plates are on the front and back pastedown endpapers, respectively.

1635. The most Pleasant § History of Tom § A Lincolne, that renowned Sol- § dier the RED-ROSE KNIGHT, who § for his Valour and Chivalry, was sirnamed § *The Boast of England.* § Shewing his Honourable Victories in Forraine § Countries, with his strange Fortunes in the *Fayrie* § Land: and how hee married the faire *Anglitora,* § Daughter to *Prester John,* that renowned § Monarke of the World. § Together with the Liues and Deaths of his two § famous Sons, the *Blacke Knight,* and the *Fayrie* § *Knight,* with diuers other memorable acci- § dents, full of delight. § [rule] § *The Seventh Impression.* § [ornament between rules] § LONDON, § Printed by *A. M.* and are to be sold by Francis Faulkner, § and Francis Coules. 1635. § *STC* 14685.

Quarto in 4s: A-M⁴. [A1] blank; A2 title; A2^v dedication; A3-G4^v text of Part One, unpaged; H title to Part Two: The Second Part § of the Famous Historie § of § TOM A LINCOLNE, § The Red-Rose Knight. § Wherein is declared his vnfortunate § Death, his Ladies Disloyaltie, his Chil- § drens Honours, and lastly his Death § most strangely reuenged. § [rule] § *Written by the first Author.* § [rule] §

[ornament] § LONDON § Printed by A. M. 1635; H^v To the Reader; H2-M4 text of Part Two unpaged; M4^v blank.

A reprint of *1631* set up page-for-page, *1635* follows it in substituting the headline "*The Bloody Letter of Queene* Caelia." for the recto half of the usual running title, "Tom a Lincolne § the Red-rose Knight." on G4. It corrects the errors in catchwords of F4^v/G, G4/G4^v, and K4 of its copy. There are no new errors in catchwords, but there are three spelling variants: B2 [-]sty,/B2^{v}stie,; C2^v Enemy/C3 Enemie; and L4^v wormes/M Wormes. The text is printed in black letter, 38 lines to the page.

The Worcester College, Oxford, copy [pressmark LR:4:4], one of three known to exist,[15] measures approximately 14.5 × 18.5 cm., and is bound in mid-sixteenth-century brown leather. It is bound between *A Saxon Historie of the Admirable Aduentures of Clodoaldvs and his three Children*: translated out of the French by Sir T. H. [Thomas Hawkins] (London, for H. Seile, 1634 [*STC* 4294]), and [Emanuel Forde], *The Most Pleasant Historie of Ornatus and Artesia* (London, B. Alsop and T. Fawcet, 1634 [*STC* 11170]).

1655. The Most Pleasant § HISTORY § OF § Tom A Lincoln, § THAT EVER RENOWNED SOULDIER § *THE* § RED-ROSE KNIGHT, § Who for his Valour and Chivalry, was Sirnamed § THE BOAST OF *ENGLAND*, § Shewing his Honourable Victories in Forrain Countries, with his strange Fortunes in the *Fayrie-Land*: and § how he married the Faire *Anglitora*, Daughter § to *Prester John*, that renowned Mo- § narck of the World. § Together with the Lives and Deaths of his two famous Sons, the § *Black Knight*, and the *Fairy Knight*, with divers other memorable § accidents, full of delight. § [rule] § *The Ninth Impression*. § [rule] § LONDON, § Printed by *T. R.* and *E. M.* for Francis Coles at the Signe of the § *Halfe-bowle* in the *Old Baily*. 1655. § Wing J807.

[15] The others are Huntington Library 62091; and Peabody Library (Baltimore) 823 J68 T.

Quarto in 4s: A-K⁴L³. [A1] title; A1ᵛ dedication; A2-Gᵛ text of Part One; G2 (missigned F2)-L3 text of Part Two, unpaged; no separate title for Part Two; To the Reader omitted.

The running title, "Tom of Lincoln § the Red-rose Knight." is invariant. There are no errors in catchwords. On C the catchword (as well as the signature) is in the last line of type. The text is in black letter, 38 lines to the page, except for speeches, which are in roman.

The Worcester College, Oxford, copy, one of two known to exist,[16] measures approximately 14.5 × 18.5 cm., and is bound in brown leather with the date 1659 stamped in gold on the spine. Also with *Tom a Lincolne* in the volume [pressmark LR:4:3] are bound the anonymous *Valentine and Orson* (London, T. Pnrfoot [sic], 1637 [*STC* 24573]); [Emanuel Forde], *Montelion* (London, B. Alsop and T. Fawcet, 1640 [Not in *STC*]); and Johnson's better-known romance, *The Seauen Champions of Christendome* (London, R. Bishop, [1639?; *STC* 14683]), *Tom a Lincolne* standing third in the volume.

Copy-Text

The text of *Tom a Lincolne* depends in the main on the unique copy of the sixth edition (1631) now in the Folger Shakespeare Library. This volume (*STC* 14684) is the earliest text of the work known to have survived, and for the reasons given below has been chosen as the copy-text for the present edition. It has been collated against one copy each of the seventh edition (1635: *STC* 14685) and of the ninth edition (1655: Wing J807), both of which copies are in the possession of Worcester College, Oxford.

The descent of the editions is as follows: the sixth (*1631*) served as the copy for the seventh (*1635*), a fairly accurate page-for-page reprint, which in turn served as the copy for the ninth (*1655*), a much less accurate reprint, either directly, or by way of the now-lost eighth. This relationship is proved both by the ornaments used in the printing of *1631* and *1635*, and by the nature of the variants throughout. The headpieces

---

[16] The other is British Museum 1077.e.57.

or ornamental initials on A3, A4, B3, C4, D4^v, G3^v, H4, I2, K4, L2, M2, and M3^v of *1631* are identical to the ones used on A2^v, A3, B2, C3, D3^v, G2^v, H2, H4, K2, K4, L4, and M^v, respectively, of *1635*. Those used on K2 and I4 of *1631* and *1635* respectively may also be identical, but the latter is so worn as to make positive identification rather difficult. In each case above, the identical ornaments are used in the same place in the text of *1635* as they were in the text of *1631*, thus proving that the compositor of *1635* had a copy of *1631* open before him while he worked. If there were any question as to the actual order of the two editions, the significantly greater wear visible in the ornaments of *1635* shows *1631* to be the earlier.

Of the ninety-one substantive variants between *1631* and *1635*, sixty-one are corruptions or modernizations, while only thirty are corrections of corrupt readings in *1631*. Of the three-hundred-thirty-seven substantive variants between *1631* and *1655*, three-hundred-two are corruptions or modernizations, forty-nine of which agree with the corresponding readings in *1635*, thus suggesting that *1635* (or an intermediary eighth edition) was its copy. *1655* corrects *1631*'s readings only thirty-five times, and twenty-five times agrees with *1635* in doing so. Of the eight indifferent or insignificant variants between *1631* and *1655* (roman numerals in place of arabic ones in chapter-headings), six of the eight agree with the corresponding readings in *1635*.

The evidence is clear. *1631* has the least corrupted text of *Tom a Lincolne* now extant, is the ultimate ancestor of all other extant texts, and is therefore the only proper choice of copy-text for a critical edition of the work.

This sixth edition of *Tom a Lincolne*, which serves as copy-text for the present edition, was probably printed line-for-line and page-for-page from a copy of the fifth, or an earlier edition. A page-for-page reprint would have made it especially easy to have had two compositors setting type simultaneously, but there is no evidence that this was done. A careful analysis of spelling variants throughout the text reveals that although certain variants do occur (such as he/hee; she/shee; maiden/mayden; faire/fayre;), they occur on the same page with each other so often that they cannot be evidence of two compositors, but only of the fact that the long form was the compositor's usual spelling, and that the short form was used to justify a crowded line.

The text of *1631* is printed in a size of black-letter type technically known as small Text. The same type size (possibly even the same fount) was used in the seventh edition as well. In both cases proper names are printed in roman in the text, and in italic in chapter-headings, which are themselves printed in roman.

One skeleton only was used in imposing the formes on the bed of the press, as is shown by the single variant headline "Tom a Lincolne." being present in every forme. Normally (in six of the eleven cases where a four-page forme printed text) the variant headline appeared on sigs. 3^v and 4^v.[17] On sheets C and F the skeleton was imposed in the reverse of the normal manner in both the outer and the inner formes, so that the variant appeared on sigs. ^{v} and 2^v in these sheets.[18] On sheet D the skeleton was imposed reversed (as on C and F) in the outer forme, but was reversed in the inner forme, so that the variant headline appeared on sigs. ^{v} and 4^v.

Later Editions

The only edition of *Tom a Lincolne* published in modern times is that edited by W. J. Thoms as part of his *Early English Prose Romances* (London, by William Pickering, 1828).[19]

In this edition Thoms merely reprinted, essentially without editing, the seventh edition (the earliest then known) from a copy lent to him by a friend, one Mr. Utterson.[20] Thoms retained the old spelling of the original, but modernized the capitalization and punctuation. He listed no variants, and probably did no collating, although he must have ex-

[17] On sheets B, E, I, K, L, M, and also (presumably) on N.

[18] Here "normal" merely means normal for this volume. As far as I know, there was no inflexible rule for the imposition of the skeleton.

[19] Reprinted 1858, 1906.

[20] Probably Edward Vernon Utterson (1776–1856).

amined at least one other edition, since he mentions that the twelfth (1682), from which he reprinted the last leaf (missing in Utterson's copy), was "much abbreviated."[21]

The Edited Text

The aim in producing this edition of *Tom a Lincolne* has been to provide a text as close as possible to what the author wrote. Time, which bears all her sons away, bore away also every copy of the first five editions of the work, leaving for copy-text but a single copy of the sixth (1631). *1631* has been collated against the seventh and ninth editions (*1635* and *1655*) and all variant readings are recorded in the Textual Notes. All emendations of *1631* are also recorded in the Textual Notes, whether drawn from *1635* and *1655* or proposed by the present editor. Long -s has been regularly modernized and the macron and ampersand silently expanded.

The most usual form of the textual note merely records a variant reading, and it therefore provides simply a lemma drawn from the precise form of the reading in the copy-text, followed by a square bracket, but omitting the siglum of the copy-text and any other text which agrees with it, which are intended to be understood. Following the bracket will be found the variant reading or readings, each followed by its siglum, and arranged in chronological order. For example, the first variant recorded involves a case in which it was decided to print the form WORTEDG from the sixth edition rather than the form WORTEDGE from the seventh and ninth editions. The note therefore reads:

WORTEDG] WORTEDGE *1635 1655*

If, as is less frequently the case, the purpose of the note is to record an emendation of the copy-text, rather than merely a variant reading, then the lemma and the square bracket will be followed by a siglum giving the source of the emendation (*1635*, *1655*, or *Ed.*), and follow-

---

[21] Thoms, p. vii.

ing a comma will be found the reading or readings which have been rejected, each with its siglum, and arranged as above.

Glosses and discussion of specific allusions and other possibly unfamiliar matters are provided in the Explanatory Notes which follow the text, and which are keyed to it by page-and-line numbers, so that a note which discusses line 11 on page 67 will be found in the notes under 67:11.

Other Versions of Tom a Lincolne

Only one other version of Johnson's work of prose fiction here edited is known to exist. This is a recently discovered MS. dramatization of Part I of *Tom a Lincolne* attributed by Mr. Peter Croft, Librarian of King's College, Cambridge, on what seems to be very cogent and convincing evidence, to Thomas Heywood (c. 1573–1641), the well-known dramatist, author of *A Woman Killed with Kindness* and many other plays; it is thought by Mr. Croft probably to have been performed as part of a Christmas entertainment at Gray's Inn.[22] The play, a unique copy of which exists in a MS. notebook owned by the Marquess of Lothian, and which was recently found among the papers of Sir John Coke (1563–1644), a Secretary of State who had connections with Gray's Inn, at Melbourne Hall, Derbyshire, is known simply as the Melbourne Hall play. The MS. is lacking the first few leaves of the first gathering, which probably contained the title, possibly other preliminaries, and almost certainly a leaf or two of the text.[23]

The MS. of the play, which occupies almost all of a notebook evidently belonging to one Morgan Evans (who signed himself "Morganus:

---

[22] *Catalogue of Autograph Letters, Historical Documents and Literary Manuscripts of the Tudor and Stuart Periods*, Sotheby, 20 November 1973, lot 72. Mr. Croft examined, read and described the Melbourne Hall MS. when it was being offered for sale by Sotheby's, of which he was then an associate. It is on this description that the section in this Introduction devoted to this important new find is based.

[23] *Ibid.*, pp. 29–34.

Evans:" at the end of the Latin "colophon" which follows the transcription of the play and who was admitted to Gray's Inn 12 June 1605) is in three distinct hands, one of which seems (by comparison with certain miscellaneous personal notes and documents of Evans' on the last few leaves of the notebook dated 1616–1619) to be that of Evans himself, and those of two others, which alternate with his frequently. It seems to have been copied in unusual circumstances, possibly clandestinely, and probably under pressure of time, as Mr. Croft concludes, sometime during the Christmas seasons of 1611 to 1615 at Gray's Inn.[24]

The play, which freely adapts Johnson's work to its own purposes, adds one main character, Rusticano, a "clown" figure who follows the hero from his humble beginnings in Lincoln right through the end of his adventures, and who provides what Mr. Croft has described as "an earthy antidote to the high-flown heroics of the knights."[25] There are also a number of additional minor characters, for example, a wife for Prester John, who drowns herself for grief when she hears of her daughter's elopement with the hero, and several rustics, friends of Tom's adoptive father, with whom he has a comic conversation, reminiscent, as Mr. Croft points out, of the first Justice Shallow scene in Shakespeare's 2 Henry IV (III.2).[26]

As must be abundantly clear by now from the notes, the present editor is indebted throughout this section to Mr. Croft, not only for comments and suggestions, but also for his kindness in providing a copy of his printed catalogue description and granting permission to quote from it. It is fervently to be hoped that the Melbourne Hall play, so long unknown, will be made available to scholars in the not-too-distant future.

The present editor is also very much indebted to Miss Jennifer Fellows, Research Student of Newnham College, Cambridge, whose question following a talk on Johnson which he gave to the James Shirley Society of St. Catharine's College, Cambridge, on 26 January 1977 first

[24] *Ibid.*, p. 29.
[25] *Ibid.*, p. 33.
[26] *Ibid.*

revealed to him the existence of the Melbourne Hall play and Mr. Croft's knowledge of it, and whose kind gift of an offprint of a fascinating note of hers, "On the Iconography of a Carving in King's College Chapel, Cambridge,"[27] illuminated for him an aspect of Johnson's *Seauen Champions* which was previously unknown to him.

[27] *Journal of the Warburg and Courtauld Institutes*, XXXIX (1976), 262.

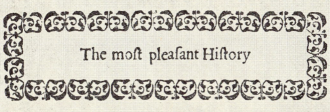

The most pleasant History

of TOM

ALINCOLNE,

That renowned Souldier, the
RED- ROSE Knight, who for
his Valour and Chivalry, was furna-
med *The Boaſt of England.*

Shewing his Honourable Victories in Forraigne
Countries, with his ſtrange Fortunes in the *Fayrie*
Land : and how he married the faire *Anglitora,*
Daughter to *Preſter Iohn,* that renowned
Monarke of the World.

Together with the Lives aud Deathes of his two
famous Sonnes, the *Blacke Knight,* and the *Fayrie
Knight,* with divers other memorable accidents, full of delight.

The ſixth Impreſſion.

LONDON,
Printed by *Aug: Mathewes* and are to bee ſold by
Robert Byrde, and *Franci: Coules.* 1631.

TO THE [A3]
RIGHT WORSHIPFVLL,
SIMON WORTEDG

of *Okenberrie* in the County of *Huntington*,
Esquire: health, happines, and prosperitie. 5

THE generall report and consideration (right Wor-
shipfull) of your exceeding courtesie, and the great
friendship which my parents haue heretofore found
at the hands of your renowned Father doe imbolden
me to present vnto your Worship these my vnpol- 10
isht Labours; which if you shall vouchsafe to cast a
fauourable glaunce vpon, and therin find any part or parcell pleasing to
your vertuous minde, I shall esteeme my trauell most highly honoured.
The History (I present) you shall finde delightfull, the matter not
offensiue to any; only my skil in penning it very simple, and my presump- 15
tion great, in presenting so rude a peece of worke to so wise a Patron;
which I hope your Worship will the more beare with, and accompt the
rather to be pardonable, in that the fault proceedeth from a good meaning.

Your worships deuoted, and
poore Country-man. 20
R. I.

3

The Pleasant Historie of

TOM A LINCOLNE,

the RED-ROSE Knight: for his

valour and Chivalrie, surnamed

the Boast of England. 5

CHAPTER I.

How King Arthur *loved faire* Angellica *the Earle of* Londons *Daughter*: *and likewise of the birth of* Tom a Lincolne.

HEN as King Arthur wore the Emperiall Diadem 10
of England, and by his chivalrie had purchased
many famous Victories, to the great renowne of
this mayden Land, hee ordeined the order of the
Round Table, and selected many worthy Knights
to attend his Maiestie: of whose glittering renowne 15
many ancient Histories doe record, and witnesse to all insuing ages.

This worthy Prince, vpon a time intending to visit the city of London, with some few number of his Knights, came and feasted with Androgius, being at that time Earle of London; whose house (as then) was
not only replenished with most delicate fare, but grac't with a number 20
of beautifull Ladyes: who gaue such a pleasing entertainement to King

5

Arthur and his Knights, that they were rauished with pleasure, and/
[A4ᵛ] quite forgot the sound of martiall Drummes, that had wont to summon
them foorth to the fields of Honour: Amongst these glorious troupes of
London Ladyes, Angellica the Earles daughter had the chiefest prayse
5 for beauty and courtly behauiour: for euen as the silver-shining Moone
in a Winters frosty night, surpasseth the brightest of the twinckling Stars:
so farre Angellicaes sweete feature exceeded the rest of the Ladyes:
whereby King Arthur was so intangled in the snares of loue, that by no
meanes he could withdraw his affections from her diuine excellence. He
10 that before delighted to tread a weary march after Bellonas Drummes,
was now constrayned to trace Cupids Measures in Ladyes Chambers: and
could as well straine the strings of a Lovers Lute, as sound a Souldiers
alarme in the field: her beauty like the Adamant, drew his steeled heart
to lodge in the closure of her breast: and no company delighted so much
15 the loue-sicke King, as the presence of faire Angellica.

So vpon a time as hee stood looking out of his Chamber window, hee
espied the Mistris of his soule sitting in a Garden under a Bower of Vines,
prettily picking the ripest Grapes with her delicate hands, and taking such
pleasant pains in that maydenlike exercise, that the well coloured blood
20 in her face began to waxe warme, and her cheeks to obtaine such an excellent beauty, that they seemed like two purple Roses intermixt with
Hawthorne-buds: whereby King Arthur grew inamored vpon her, and
stood for a time sencelesse through the extreame passion he tooke in beholding her beauty: But at last recouering his senses, he spake to himself in
25 this manner.

Oh most diuine Angellica, Natures sole wonder, thou excellent orna-
ment of Beauty, thy louely Face painted with a crimson die, thy rosieall
Cheekes surpasing Snow in whitenesse, thy decent Necke like purest
Iuory, hath like a Fowlers net intangled my yeelding heart: whereby it
30 is for euermore imprisoned in thy breast. Oh that the golden Tresses of
thy dainty Haire which shine like the Rubyes, glittering in the Sunne,
had neuer twinckled before my rauisht eyes, then had my heart inioyed
his wonted liberty, and my Fancie been free from Lovers vaine imaginations. Thus, and in like manner, complayned the King vnto himselfe,

6

seeking by all meanes/possible to exclude Loues fire from his breast. But [B]
the more hee stroue to abandon it, the more it increased: and feeling no
pollicie might preuaile, but that this burning torment must of force bee
quenched with her celestiall loue hee descended from his Chamber, and
went bouldly into the Garden; where taking Angellica by the hand as   5
shee sate vpon a bed of Violets, which as then grew vnder the Arbour, in
this manner began to court her.

    Faire of all faires, (sayd the King) deuine and beautious Paragon,
faire Flower of London, know that since my aboad in thy Fathers house,
thy beauty hath so conquered my affections, and so bereaued me of my 10
liberty, that vnlesse thou vouchsafe to coole my ardent desires with a willing graunt of thy loue, I am like to dye a languishing death, and this
Countrey England of force must loose him, that hath filde her boundes
with many triumphant Victories: therefore sweet Angellica, if thy hard
heart be so obdurate, that the teares of my true loue may nothing mollifie, 15
yet take pitty on thy Countrey that through thy cruelty, she loose not her
wonted glory, and be made vnhappy, by the losse of her Soueraigne: thou
seest (my diuine Angellica) how I, that haue made Princes stoope, and
Kings to humble when I haue frownde, doe now submissiuely yeeld my
high honour to thy feete, either to be made happy by thy loue, or vnhappy 20
in thy hate, that in time to come, Children may either blesse, or curse thee:
Of these two, consider which thou wilt performe either with cruelty to
kill mee or with clemencie to preserue mee.

    This vnexpected request of the King, so amazed Angellica, that her
Cheeks were stayned with blushing shame, and like a bashfull Maiden 25
(for a time) stood silent not knowing in what manner to answere him,
considering hee was King of England, and she but Daughter to an Earle:
But at last, when feare and shame had awhile stroue together in her heart,
shee replyed in this sort.

    Most mighty King (said shee) if your entertainement in my Fathers 30
house hath beene honourable, seeke not the foule dishonour of his Daughter, nor proffer to blemish the bud of her virginitie with the least thought
of your vnchast desires: the losse/of which sweet Iemme, is a torment to [Bᵛ]
my soule more worse then death. Consider with your selfe (most worthy

Prince) the blacke scandall that it may bring vnto your name and honour, hauing a Queene, a most vertuous and loyall Princesse. Thinke vpon the staine of your mariage bed, the wrongs of your wedded pheere, and lasting infamie of your owne glorie, for this I vow (by Dianaes bright ma-
5 iesty) before I will yeeld the conquest of my virginitie to the spoyle of such vnchast desires, I will suffer more torments, than mans heart can imagine: therefore (most mighty Soueraigne) cease your vnreuerend suite, for I will not loose that matchlesse Iewell, for all the treasure the large Ocean containes: And in speaking these words shee departed thence,
10 and left the loue-sicke King in the Arbour, complaining to the emptie ayre: where after hee had numbred many determinations together, this hee purposed: Neuer to cease his suite, till he had gained what his soule so much desired: for continually at the break of day, when Titans beautie began to shine, and Auroraes blush to appeare, would hee alwayes send to
15 her Chamber window the sweetest Musicke that could bee deuised: thinking thereby to obtaine her Loue. Many times would hee solicite her with rich gifts, and large promises, befitting rather an Empresse then the Daughter of an Earle, profering such kindnes, that if she had a heart of Iron, yet could shee not choose but relent and requite his curtesies: for
20 what is it that time will not accomplish, hauing the hand of a King set thereunto.

Twelue weary dayes King Arthur spent in woing of Angellica, before hee could obtaine his hearts happinesse, and his soules content: at the end of which time, she was as plyant to his will, as is the tender twig to
25 the hand of the Husbandman. But now their secret meaning required a pollicie to keepe their priuie loues both from King Arthurs Queene, and from old Androgius, Angellicas Father: and that their secret ioyes might long time continue without mistrust of any partie whatsoeuer, this deuice they contriued: that Angellica should desire liberty of her Father, to
30 spend the remaine of her life in the service of Diana, like one that abandoned all earthly vanitie, honouring true chastity and religious life: So,
[B₂] with a/demure countenance, and a sober grace, shee went vnto her Father, and obtained such leaue at his hands, that he willingly condiscended that shee should liue as a professed Nunne, in a Monasterie that

8

the King before time had builded in the Citie of Lincolne; and so furnishing her foorth with such necessaries as her state required, he gaue her his blessing, and so committed her to Dianaes seruice.

But now Angellica being no sooner placed in the Monastery and chosen a Sister of that fellowship, but King Arthur many times visited 5 her in so secret a manner, and so disguisedly, that no man suspected their pleasant meetings: but so long tasted they the ioyes of loue, that in the end the Nunne grew great bellied, and bore King Arthurs quittance sealed in her wombe, and at the end of forty weekes, shee was deliuered; where in presence of the Midwife, and one more whom the King largly recom- 10 penced for their secrecy, shee was made a happy Mother of a goodly sonne, whom King Arthur caused to be wrapped in a Mantle of greene Silke, tying a Purse of Gold about his necke, and so causing the Midwife to beare it into the Fields, and to lay it at a Shepheards gate neere adioyning to the Citie, in hope the old man should foster it as his own: by which 15 means his Angellicaes dishonour might be kept secret from the world, and his owne disgrace from the murmuring reports of the vulgar people.

This his commandement was so speedily performed by the Midwife, that the very next morning she stole the young Infant from his Mothers keeping, and bore it secretly to the place appointed, there laying it downe 20 vpon a turffe of greene grasse: it seemed prettily to smile, turning his christall eyes vp towards the Elements, as though it foreknew his owne good Fortune. This being done, the Midwife withdrew her selfe some little distance from that place, and hid her selfe closely behind a well growne Oake, diligently marking what should betide the comfortlesse 25 Infant: But long shee had not there remained, but there flocked such a number of little Birdes about the young harmelesse Babe, and made such a chirping melody, that it fell into a silent slumber, and slept as sweetly as though it had been layde in a Bed of softest Silke.

By this time, the golden Sunne began to glister on the/Mountaine [B2ᵛ] top, and his sister Luna to withdraw her waterish countenance: at which time, the pleasant Shepheards began to tune their Morning notes, and to repayre vnto their foulded Sheepe, according to their woonted manner: Amongst which crue of lusty Swaines, old Antonio approached foorth of

9

his Gate with a chearefull countenance, whose Beard was as white as polished Siluer, or like to Snow lying vpon the Northerne Mountaines: this bonny Shepheard no sooner espied Angelicaes sweet Babe lying vpon the greene Hillocke, but immediatly hee tooke it vp; and viewing circum-
5 spectly euery parcell of the rich Vestments wherein it was wrapped, at last found out the Purse of Gold which the King had tyed vnto the Childs necke, whereat the Shepheard so exceedingly reioyced, that for the time, he stoode as a man rauished with pleasure, and was not able to re-moue from the place where he stood: but yet at the last, thinking with
10 himselfe that Heauen had sent him that good fortune, not onely giuing him Riches, but withall a Sonne, to be a comfort to him in his latter yeares; so bearing it in to his old Wife, and withall the Purse of Gold, and the rich Mantle, with the other things: who at the sight thereof, was as highly pleased as her Husband, when he found it first: so being both
15 agreed to foster and bring it vp as their own, considering that Nature neuer gaue them in all their life any child, incontinently they caused it to be christened, and called by the name of TOM A LINCOLNE; (after the Towne where it was found) a name most fitting for it, in that they knew not who were his true Parents.
20   But now speake wee againe of the Midwife, that after shee had be-held how kindly old Antonio receiued the young Infant, shee returned backe unto Angelicaes Chamber, whom shee found bitterly lamenting the losse of her tender Babe, thinking that some Fayry Nimph had stolne it away: but such was the kind comfort which the smooth-tonged Midwife
25 gaue her in that extremity, whereby her sorrow seemed the lesse, and her mistrustfull feare exchanged into smiling hope: yet neither would the King nor the Midwife at any time whatsoeuer, make knowne vnto her what was become of her little Sonne, but driuing her off with delayes and
[B3] fond excuses, lest hauing intelligence of his/aboad, she should (through
30 kinde loue, and naturall affection) goe visite him, and so discouer their Loues practises.
     Thus liued the most fayre Angelica many dayes in great griefe, wish-ing his returne, and desiring Heauen that the Destinies might be so fa-uourable, that once againe before the fatall Sisters had finished her life,

she might behold her Infants face: for whose presence her very soule thirsted.

Here will we leaue the solitary Lady comfortlesse and without company (except it were the King, that sometimes visited her by stealth) and report what happened to Tom a Lincolne in the Shepheards house. 5

CHAPTER II.

Of the manner of Tom a Lincolnes *bringing vp, and how he first came to be called* the RED-ROSE Knight: *with other things that hapned to him.* 10

GREAT WAS THE WEALTH that old Antonio gathered together, by meanes of the Treasure hee found about the Infants attire, whereby hee became the richest in all that Country, and purchast such Lands and Liuings, that his supposed Sonne (for wealth) was deemed a fit match for a Knights Daughter: Yet for all this his bringing vp was but meane, 15 and in a homely sort; for after he had passed ten yeares of his age hee was set to keepe Antonioes Sheepe, and to follow Husbandry, whereby he grew strong and hardy, and continually gaue himselfe to painefull endeauours, imagining and deuising haughty and great enterprises: yet notwithstanding was of honest and vertuous conditions, well featured, val- 20 iant, actiue, quick and nimble, sharpe witted, and of a ripe iudgement: hee was of a valiant and inuincible courage, so that from his Cradle and infancie, it seemed he was vowed to Mars, and martiall exploits. And in his life and manners is deciphered the Image of true Nobilitie: for though hee obscurely liued in a Countrey Cottage, yet had he a superiour mind, aim- 25 ing at state and maie/stie, bearing in his breast the princely thoughts of [B3ᵛ] his Father. For on a time keeping Cattell in the Field amongst other yong men of his age and condition, he was chosen (in sport by them) for their Lord or Knight, and they to attend on him like dutifull Seruants: and although this their election was but in play, yet he whose spirits were 30

I I

rauished with great and high matters, first, procured them to sweare to him loyalty in all things; and to obey him as a King, where, or when it should please him in any matter to command them: to which they all most willingly condescended. Thus after they had solemnly taken their
5 oathes, he perswaded them to leaue that base and seruile kind of life, seeking to serue in Warre, and to follow him, being the Generall: the which through perswasion they did, and so leauing their Cattell to their Fathers and Masters, they assembled all together, to the full number of a hundred at the least: vnto whom he seuerally gaue certaine Red Roses,
10 to be worne for colours in their Hattes, and commanded them, that euer after hee should be called the Red-rose Knight. So in this manner departed he with his followers vnto Barnsedale Heath, where they pitched vp Tents, and liued long time vpon the robberies and spoyles of passengers, in so much that the whole Country were greatly molested by them.
15   This disordered life so highly displeased the Parents of these vnruly Outlawes, that many of them died with griefe: but especially of all other, old Antonio tooke it in ill part, considering how dearely hee loued him, and how tenderly hee brought him vp from his infancy: therefore he purposed to practise a meane to call him from that vnciuill kinde of life, if it
20 might possible be brought to passe: so in his old dayes vndertaking this taske, hee trauelled towards Barnsedale Heath: into which being no sooner entred but some of the ruder sort of these Outlawes ceased vpon the old man, and without any further violence, brought him before their Lord and Captain: who at the first sight knew him to be his Father (as
25 he thought) and therefore vsed him most kindly, giuing him the best entertainement that hee could deuise: where, after they had some small time conferred together, the good old man brake out into these speeches.
[B4]   Oh thou degenerate (quoth he) from natures kind: Is this thy duty to thy fathers age, thus disobediently to liue, wounding thy naturall
30 Countrey with vnlawfull spoyles? Is this the comfort of mine age: is this thy loue vnto thy Parents, whose tender care hath been euer to aduance thy estate? Canst thou behold these milke-white Hayres of mine all to rent and torne, which I haue violently martyred in thy absence? Canst thou indure to see my dim Eyes almost sightlesse through age, to

12

drop downe Teares at thy disobedient feete? Oh wherefore hast thou infringed the Lawes of Nature, thus cruelly to kill thy fathers heart with
griefe, and to end his dayes by thy vitious life? Returne, returne deare
Child, banish from thy breast these base actions, that I may say, I haue a
vertuous Sonne: and be not like the viperous brood, that workes the vn-   5
timely death of their Parents. And speaking these words, griefe so exceeded the bounds of Reason, that hee stood silent, and beginning againe
to speake, teares trickled from his eyes in such abundance, that they stayed
the passage of his speech: the which being perceiued by the Red-rose
Knight, he humbly fell vpon his knees, and in this sort spake vnto good   10
Antonio.

Most deare and reuerent Father, if my offence doe seeme odious in
your eyes, that I deserue no forgiuenesse then here behold now your poore
inglorious Sonne, laying his breast open, ready prepared to receiue Deaths
remorselesse stroke from your aged hands, as a due punishment for this   15
my disobedient crime: but to be reclaimed from this honourable kind of
life (I count it honourable because it tasteth of manhood), first shall the
Sun bring day from out the Westerne Heauens, and the siluer Moone
lodge her brightnesse in the Easterne waues, and all things else against
both kind and nature turne their wonted course.   20

Well then (quoth Antonio) if thy resolution bee such, that neither
my bitter teares, nor my faire intreaties may preuaile to withdraw thy
vaine folly, then know (thou most vngratious impe) that thou art no
Sonne of mine, but sprung from the bowels of some vntamed Tyger, or
wild Lionesse, else wouldst thou humbly submit thy selfe to my reuerent   25
perswasions; from whence thou camest I know not, but sure thy breast
harbours the tyranny of some monstrous Tyrant, from whose loynes/thou [B4ᵛ]
art naturally descended. Thou art no fruite of my body for I found thee
(in thy infancy) lying in the Fields, cast out as a prey for rauening
Fowles, ready to bee deuowred by hunger-starued Dogges: but such was   30
my pitty towards thee, that I tooke thee vp and euer since haue fostered
thee as mine owne Child: but now, such is thy vnbridled folly, that my
kind curtesie is requited with extreame ingratitude; which sinne aboue
all others, the immortall powers of Heauen doe condemne, and the very

13

Diuels themselues doe hate: therefore like a Serpent, henceforth will I spit at thee, and neuer cease to make incessant prayers to the iustfull Heauens, to reuenge this thy monstrous disobedience.

These words being ended, hee gaue such an extreame sigh, that his 5 very heart brake with griefe, and hee immediatly dyed in the presence of the Red-rose Knight. For whose death, hee made more sorrowfull lamentation, then Niobe did for her seuen Sonnes. But in recompence of old Antonioes kind loue, that preserued his infancie from the fury of rauenous Fowles, he intombed him most stately in the Citie of Lincolne, 10 whose body he sent thither by certaine Passengers whom hee had taken, and withall a thousand pound in treasures, to be bestowed vpon a great Bell to bee rung at his Funerall, which Bell hee caused to bee called Tom a Lincolne after his owne name, where to this day it remaineth in the same Citie: These Passengers being as then rich Merchants of London 15 hauing receiued the dead body of old Antonio, and withall the treasure, went with all speed vnto Lincolne, and performed euery thing as the Red-rose Knight had appointed.

The death of this good old man not onely caused a generall sorrow through the whole Citie, but stroke such an extreame griefe to old An-20 tonioes wife, that shee within few dayes yeelded her life to the remorce-lesse stroke of the frowning destinies, and was buried in the same graue where her Husband was intombed: Whose deaths we will now leaue to be mourned by their dearest friends, and likewise for breuities sake, passe ouer many stratagems which were accomplished by the Red-rose Knight 25 and his followers vpon Barnsedale Heath, and returne to King Arthur and his Knights, flourishing in the English Court.

[C]

CHAPTER III.

Of the first Conquest of Portingale *by the* Red-ROSE Knight, *and how hee was the* first that
30 euer triumphed *in the* Citie of London.

THE REPORT of Tom a Lincolnes practises grew so generall amongst the vulgar sort of people, that at last it came to king Arthurs eares, who imagined in his Princely minde, that he was sprung of his bloud, and that hee carried lofty thoughts of honour planted in his breast, though shrowded vnder a Countrey life: therefore through kinde nature, hee purposed to haue him resident in Court with him, that hee might daily see his liuely sparkes of honour shew their resplendant brightnesse, yet 5 in such obscurity, that hee should not know the smallest motion of his Parentage; therefore hee called together three of his approoued Knights, namely Lancelot du Lake, Sir Tristram and Sir Triamore, and gaue them in charge, if it were possible, to fetch the Red-rose Knight vnto his Court, of whose aduenturous exploits hee hath heard so many times re- 10 ported: and withall he gaue them generall Pardon, sealed with his priuie Seale, for him and all his lawlesse followers.

This Commission beeing receiued by the three worthie Knights, they with all speede armed themselues in rich Corselets, and strong habiliments of Warre, and so rode towards Barnsedale Heath where being no 15 sooner come, and deliuered their message from the King, but the Redrose Knight gaue them an honourable welcome, and for three dayes most royally feasted them vnder large Canuasse Tents; wherein they slept as securely, as they had beene in King Arthurs Court, or in a strong Castle of warre. 20

After this, Tom a Lincolne selected out a hundred of his resolute Followers, such as he best liked of, and came with Sir Lancelot, and the rest to the English Court; where King Arthur/not onely gaue him a [Cᵛ] friendly entertainment, but also installed him one of his Knights of the Round-table: and withall proclaimed a solemne Turniament, that 25 should be holden in the honour of this new made Knight: to which Turniament, assembled from other Countries, many Princes, Barons, and Knights of high honour, which behaued themselues most nobly, and woon great commendations of euery beholder: but especially the Red-rose Knight, who for that day, stood as chiefe Champion against all commers. 30 In that Turniament, or first dayes deede of his Knighthood, where onely by his valour and prowesse hee ouerthrew three Kings, and thirty other Knights, all famouzed for Chivalry: whereby he obtained such grace in the English Court, that he had by the King a paire of golden Spurres put

15

vpon his feet, and generally of the whole assembly, he was accounted one of the brauest Knights that then liued in the world.

But now marke, how frowning Fortune ended their Triumphes with vnlucky Newes: for the same day before the Knights had vnbuckled
5 their Armours, there arriued a Messenger, who certified King Arthur, how his Ambassadour was vniustly done to death in the Portingale Court, (which was an Act contrary both to the Faith of Princes, and the Law of Armes:) For whose death King Arthur grew so enraged, that he sware by the Honour of his bright Renowne, and by the golden Spurre of true
10 Knighthood, the Portingales should repent that inhumane violence, with the death of many thousand guiltlesse soules; and that Babes vnborne, should haue iust cause to curse the first contriuer of that vniust murther: therefore with all speede hee mustered vp a mighty Armie of Souldiers, and (because hee was continually molested with home-bred Mutinies,
15 and treacherous rebellions, the which himselfe in person of force must pacifie) appointed the Red-rose Knight as chiefe Generall ouer the Armie mustered for Portingale. In which Seruice, hee accomplished so many famous Exployts, that hee was for euer after surnamed, The Boast of England. For no sooner had hee the whole Campe in charge, and
20 aboard their Shippes, but hee prooued the perfect Patterne of an exquisite Souldier: such a one, as all martiall Captaines may learne to imitate: for
[C2] hee so circumspectly ordered his Captaines, that/in his Campe was neuer knowne any brawle or mutenie. He was very courteous and liberall, doing honour to all men according to their deserts. He so painfully and with such
25 care instructed his Souldiers, that at an instant alwayes (if it were need-full) euery man by the sound of a Drumme or a Trumpet, was found in his Charge and Quarter. And (to be briefe) his Campe resembled one of the greatest Cities in the world, for all kind of officers were there found in order: and also a great number of Merchants to furnish it with all
30 manner of necessaryes. He in no case permitted any robberies, priuy fighting, force, or violence: but with seuerity punished those that were therein found guiltie. His desire was, that his Souldiers should glory in nothing so much, as in Martiall prowesse, Vertue, and Wisedome. He euermore gaue them their pay without fraud or deceit. He honoured, he

praysed, he imbrac'd and kist them, and withall kept them in awe and subiection: by which meanes his fame and honour grew so renowned, that his Army dayly encreased more and more. For when he first arriued vpon the Confines of Portingale, his Campe grew to bee as great as euer was Caesars, when he conquered the Western World, and in matchlesse 5 prowesse nothing inferiour vnto his. So fortunate were his proceedings, that he made a great part of the Prouinces of Portingale desolate, not being intercepted by any, but spoyling euery Towne and Citie as hee went, vntill such time as the Portingale King had gathered together a marvailous number of Souldiers, both olde, and of much experience, by reason 10 of the continuall Warres that they had with the Turkish Nation adioyning neere vnto them: But when this Portingale King (like an expert Souldier) seeing that no way he might resist the English Army, nor expell them his Countrey, vnlesse he gaue them present Battaile, therefore trusting in his approued Manhood, and the prowesse of his Souldiers, he 15 set his Army in a readinesse and so marched forward to meet the Red-rose Knight, and his warlike followers, which at that time had pitched his Campe in a large Champion Plaine, adioyning neere vnto the Citie of Lishborne, whereat both these Armies met: and setting them in order (as it became good Captaines) there they began (in the breake of/the day) [C2ᵛ] the most cruell and terriblest Battle that euer was heard of, or fought in that age, considering the number of both parties, their experience and pollicy, with the valiant courage and prowesse of their Captaines.

In great danger continued this fight, till the Sun beganne to set, with marveilous slaughter on both sides; yet remayned the victory doubtfull, 25 declining neither to the Portingales, nor yet to the English: but at last (though long) the Portingales began to faint and flie; more indeed opprest with the multitude then for any feare they receiued in the Battell, for the most part of them with honour dyed manfully in the Field, some taken prisoners, and the rest fled for their better safety: but now the Por- 30 tingale King perceiuing his Souldiers begin to flye, with courage hee sought to withdraw them from flight, resisted in person valiantly the furious rage of the enemy: but in that enterprise he gained such and so many knockes, that at last hee was vnhorst, and for want of reskew, was

forst to yeeld himselfe as prisoner: whereat the whole armie of the Portingales were discomfeited, and the victory fell to the Englishmen: the
which being obtayned, the Red-rose Knight with his Armie entred into
the Citie of Lishborne; where the common Souldiers were inriched with
5 wealthy spoyles, and the Kings Pallace ransacked by the Red-rose
Knight; where hee tooke such prisoners as him best liked, and the rest
(like an honorable souldier) he sat at liberty, commaunding that no violence should be proffered any way.

After this, setting his Army in a readinesse, he marched towards
10 England, where after some few dayes trauell, hee arriued with all his
Hoast, in the Westerne parts of Deuonshire, and marching towards London, where against his comming, the Citizens with the Inhabitants of
other villages neere adioyning, were that day seene in their most sumptuous and rich attire, euery one of them endeauoring to place himselfe
15 in some Gallery or Window, that the better and with more ease they
might behold the triumphant returne of the Red-rose Knight. All the
Churches in London were on euery side set open, hanged round about
with most costly forniture: the streetes were also most gloriously beset
[C3] with greene Boughes, and strowed/with Perfumes of no small value:
20 and for the infinite multitude of people that were seene in the Citie, there
were appointed a hundred Whiflers most richly attyred to keepe the
streets plaine and open, whereby the triumphs might haue the easier passage: and for that the diuersity of the shewes were so many, that they of
necessitie were constrained to part them into three seuerall dayes.

25 The first day hardly sufficed in good order to bring in the Banners,
Standards, and Ensignes of the Conqueror, the golden Images, and
Tables of price, which were all brought in on Carts very curiously painted
and trimmed.

On the second day, came in the Armour of the Conquered King, as
30 also of all the other Portingale Lords: and as they were rich, bright, and
glittering, so were they with most cunning ordered and couched in wag-
gons. After these entred three thousand men, in order, bearing nothing but
Money openly to bee seene, and that in huge Platters and Vessels of Siluer; of which were three hundred and fiftie in number, and foure of our

18

men allotted to euery vessell: the other brought in most artificiall Tapestry works, beautified with gold and siluer. And thus was the second dayes Triumph ended, in most pompous solemnitie.

Vpon the third day, euen at the rising of the Sunne, with the first Band, entred (as a ioyfull sound of Conquest) an infinite number of 5 Flutes, Drummes, and Trumpets, with other like Martiall and Warlike Instruments, sounding not after a most pleasant and sweet manner, but in most terrible sort, as it was possible to be done, euen in such order as they doe, when they presently ioyne Battaile. And after them, came a hundred and twentie Kine all white, hauing their Hornes curiously 10 gilded with Gold, their bodies couered with Vayles, (which they accompted most sacred and holy) bearing also Garlands of Flowers vpon their Heads, driuen by certaine young Gentlemen, no lesse well fauoured then gorgeously attyred. After these, followed the Coach of the conquered King of Portingale, with his owne Armour layd thereon openly 15 to bee seene of all men: his Crowne and royall Scepter was layd in seemely order vpon his Armour. After his Coach,/came Prisoners on foot, with [C3ᵛ] his owne naturall Children, being little Infants: and after them followed a great Troup of his Seruants and Officers, as Masters of his Houshould, Secretaries, Ushers, Controlers, Chamberlaines, with other Gentlemen 20 of his Court, all in a most sorrowfull manner, seeing themselues brought into such extremitie and seruitude, that they mooued to compassion all such as beheld them. Of the Kings children, there were two Boyes, and one Girle, of age so young and tender, that they had small vnderstanding of their misfortune and misery. 25

In this triumph followed the Father his owne Children, (after the vsage of his Countrey) clad in black mourning garments, sorrowing likewise for his hard misfortune. Then followed sundry of his approoued Friends: which, beholding in that plight their vnhappy Prince, brake out into teares and sighes so bitterly, that their enemies themselues grieued 30 at their mishaps.

After these, followed one which carryed certaine precious Stones, that had been presented to the Red-rose Knight, from some ancient Cities in Portingale, who immediatly followed in person triumphantly in his

19

Iuory Chariot, apparelled in vestures of purple Tissue, hauing a Lawrell bough in his hand, and a Crowne of the same vpon his Head. After him, followed his owne Souldiers, both foot-men, and Horse-men, all marching in most decent order, armed with rich Furniture, holding also each
5 of them a Lawrell bough in his hand, their Ensignes and Banners Souldier-like displayed, sounding Martiall Melody in honour of their triumphant Captain: with many other like presidents, most royall and magnificent.

Thus in this gallant order marched they to the Kings Chappell,
10 where in the presence of the King and his Lords, (which came to honour and grace their Triumphs) they gaue thanks to God for their successfull victory: where after solemne Seruice was ended, they departed to King Arthurs Court, where euery one, as well Strangers as others, were most royally feasted.

15 The Portingale King seeing his kind entertainement in the English
[C4] Court, where he was vsed more like a Friend, then an/Enemie had small care to returne home, but frolik'd many a day amongst the English Lords: whose loues vnto strangers be euermore most honourable. But so great were the courtesies that the Noble King Arthur bestowed vpon
20 the Portingales, who for their proffered disgraces, requited them liberally with honour: and not onely sent them home ransomlesse, but promised to lend them ayde and succour from England, if occasion required. So bearing them company to the Sea side, hee most friendly committed them to the mercy of the winds and waues, which were so fauourable, that in
25 short time they arriued safe in their owne Country; where many a day after they remembred the honourable kindnesse of the English-men, and caused the Chronicles of Portingale to record the renowne of King Arthur, and his Knights of the Round Table.

CHAPTER IIII.

How the Red-ROSE *Knight trauelled from the* King of Englands Court, *and how he arriued in the* Fayerie-land, *where he was entertained by a* Mayden Queene, *and what* $_5$
happened to him in the same Country.

NOW, after the Portingales were thus conquered, and sent home with great honour, the English King and his Lordes, rested themselues many a day in the Bowers of Peace, leauing their Armours rusting, and their pampered Steedes standing in their Stables, forgetting their vsuall man- 10 ner of wrathfull warre: which idle ease greatly discontented the magnanimious Red-rose Knight, who thought it a staine to his passed glory, and a scandall to his Princely mind to entertaine such base thoughts: and considering with himselfe how ignorant hee was of his true Parents, and from whence hee was descended, hee could not imagine: therefore hee 15 purposed to begin a new enterprise, and so trauaile vp and downe the World, till hee had either/found his Father and Mother, or else yeelded [C4ᵛ] his life to Natures course in that pretended Iourney: so going to the King, (full little thinking that he was sprung from so Noble a stock) crauing at his Graces hand, to graunt him such liberty, for to try his Knight-hood 20 in forraine Countries, whereas yet did neuer Englishman make his aduenture; and so eternize his name to all posterity, rather then to spend his life in such home-bred practises.

To this his honourable request, the King (though loath to forgoe his company, yet because it belonged to Knightly Attempts) hee gaue him 25 leaue, and withall, furnished him a Shippe at his owne proper cost and charges, giuing free Licence to all Knights whatsoeuer, to beare him company: amongst which number, Sir Launcelot du Lake was the chiefest that preferred himselfe to that Voyage, who protested such loue to the Red-rose Knight, that they plighted their Faiths like sworne Brothers, 30 and to liue and die together in all extreamities.

So these two English Knights, with the number of a hundred more,

all resolute Gentlemen, tooke leaue of the King, and with all speede
went a Ship-boord: wherein being no sooner entred, but the Pylot hoysed
Sayle and disanchored, and so committed their liues and Fortunes to the
pleasure of Neptunes mercie: vpon whose watry kingdome they had not
5 many dayes sayled, but Aeolus brazen gates burst open, and the Windes
so violently troubled the swelling waues, that euery minute they were in
danger, to end their liues in the bottome of the Seas.

Three moneths the winde and the waters stroue together for suprem-
acie: during which time, they sawe no land, but were driuen vp and
10 downe, to what place the euer-changing Destenies listed: so at last they
sayled beyond the Sunne, directed only by the light of the Starres, not
knowing which way to trauell towards land, but in such extremity for
want of Victuall, that they were forced to land at a certaine Iland in the
Westerne parts of the world, inhabited onely by women: where being no
15 sooner on land, and giuing God thanks for deliuering them from that
[D] mortall perill, but the Red-rose Knight cast vp/his eyes towards the
higher parts of the Countrey, and espied more then two thousand women
comming foorth at a Citie gate, all most richly armed with Breast-plates
of Siluer, marching in trim aray, like an Army of well approoued Soul-
20 diers: the which number comming neere to the Sea side, they sent two of
their Damsels, as Messengers to the English Knights, willing them, as
they loued their liues, presently to retire againe back to the Seas, for that
was no Countrey for their abode. But when the Red-rose Knight of England had vnderstoode the bold message of the two Damsels, he was sore
25 abashed (considering the number of armed women he saw before him,
and the great dangers they had suffered before on the Sea for want of
victuals) that he knew not in what manner he were best to answere them:
but hauing a good courage, hee at last spake to the two Damsels in this
sort.

30 Right Noble Ladies, I haue well vnderstood your speeches: therefore
I desire you for to shew such fauour vnto wandering Trauailers, as to
tell vs in what Country Fortune hath brought vs to: and for what cause
we are commanded by you to returne to the Sea?

Surely Sir Knight (answered one of the Damsels) this Countrey

22

whereon you are ariued, it is not very bigge, but yet most fertile and
commodious; and is called by the name of the Fayrie-Land: And now to
shew you the cause why you are commaunded to returne, this it is. Not
many yeares agoe, there raigned in this Countrey a King which had to
name Larmos, for wisedome and prowesse not his equall was found in   5
any of these parts of the world. This King had such continuall warre
against the bordering Ilanders, that vpon a time he was constrained to
muster for the same warre all the men both young and old which were
found in this Kingdome, whereby the whole Countrey was left destitute
of men, to the great discontentment of the Ladies and Damsels that here   10
inhabited: whereupon they finding themselues so highly wronged, liuing
without the company of men, they generally assembled themselues together, with the Daughter of King Larmos, which is called Caelia, no
lesse in Beautie, then in Vertue and Wisedome: These Ladyes and
Damosels beeing gathered toge/ther, with a generall consent, dispatched   [D^v]
certaine Messengers to the King, and to their Husbands, willing them to
returne into their Countrey, and not to leaue their wiues and children in
such extremity, without the comfort and company of man. Vpon which,
the King answered, that hee had besieged his Enemies in their Townes of
Warre; and before one man should returne home till he came with Con-   20
quest, his Country should bee lost and made desolate, and the Women
giuen ouer to the spoyle of his Enemies: Which answere, when the Ladies
had receiued, they tooke it in such euill part, that they conspired against
their King, and Husbands, and put to death all the men children that
were in the Countrey; and after determined, when their Husbands, Fa-   25
thers, and Friends returned from the Warre, that they should the first
night of their comming, bee slaine sleeping in their Beds, and that neuer
after they should suffer man to enter into their Countrey. After this conclusion, they crowned Caelia the Kings Daughter for their Queene: and
so afterward, when the King and his Armie returned from his Warres,   30
this bloudy Murther was practised, and not a man left aliue, but onely
the King reserued, whom Caelia would in no wise against nature murther: but yet notwithstanding, shee deliuered him into the hands of her
chiefest Ladies, which put him into a Boat alone, and so sent him to the

Sea to seeke his fortune. Therefore most noble Knights, this is the cause, why you may not enter into our Countrey: which if you doe, and not presently withdraw your selues vnto the Sea, the Ladies will suddenly giue you a meruailous Battell.

5   Now by the Euer-liuing God, which English-men adore, (said the Noble Red-rose Knight) such extremitie haue wee suffered at Sea, that wee are like to perish and dye with hunger, vnlesse wee finde some suc-cour at your hands: and before we will end our liues with famine, we will enter Battell with those Ladies, and so dye with Honour in the Field:

10   yet this kindnesse doe we humbly desire at your hands, to returne vnto your Queene, and certifie her of our poore estate and necessity, and that we altogether instantly desire her, that if there be any sparke of Vertue,

[D2] or Nobility harboured in her breast, that shee/will haue pitie vpon vs, and suffer vs not to end our liues by such an vnhappy kinde of death.

15   With this request the two Damsels returned to the Queen and re-counted from word to word the humble suit of the Red-rose Knight, and what extremitie they were in: Which when the Queene vnderstood, and that they were Knights of England, the fame of which countrey shee had so often heard reported, shee demaunded, what manner of people

20   they were, and of what condition? Surely Madam (answered one of the two Damsels) I neuer in all my life saw more goodly men, nor better spoken: and it is to bee supposed, they bee the choyce of all humane people, and with their courteous demeanors, are able to drawe the mercilesse and sauage Nation to affect them.

25   The Queene hearing the Damsels so highly to commend the English Knights, thinking also vpon their request, began (in minde) to haue pitie of their misaduentures, and so instantly sent for them, and gaue them free libertie to make their abode in her Countrey: which incontinently when the English Knights heard, how they should receiue a kinde wel-

30   come, and a friendly entertainment, grew so exceeding ioyfull, as though Heauen had sent them present comfort: so comming before the Queene and her Ladyes, they saluted each other most courteously, and with great reuerence. But when the vertuous Queene behelde this noble company before her, in all humilitie, shee deliuered to a hundred of her

Ladies, the hundred English Knights, and reserued the Princely Red-rose Knight vnto her selfe: and so were they brought to the Queenes Pallace, where euery Lady feasted her Knight in most gallant sort, and to their hearts content. But now when the Queene had the Red-rose Knight in her Chamber, and had beheld the exceeding beautie of the 5 noble Prince, shee tooke him by the hand, and led him into one of her Chambers, where she shewed him her Riches and Treasure: and after sayd vnto him in this manner.

Most noble and valiant Englishman, these Riches bee all onely at thy Commandement, and also my body, which here I offer vp as a gift 10 and Present to thy diuine excellencie: and / furthermore, there is nothing [D2ᵛ] of value, which I am Mistris of, but shall be at thy disposing, to the intent that my loue may be acceptable to thy gracious eyes. But when the Red-rose Knight perceiued to what intent she spake these words, in this manner answered her, saying. 15

Most deare Princesse, and faire Queene of this Maiden countrey, I giue you right humble thankes for these your courtesies, and by no meanes possible may I deserue this high honour you haue grac'd me with.

Oh great Knight (replyed then the Queene) the smallest thought of your honourable minde, is sufficient to recompence the vttermost of my 20 deserts: yet let me request this one thing at your noble hands, that neuer asked the like fauour of anyone before, for she that neuer knew the least motion of loue, is now pricked with a hundred torments: and vnlesse you quench the ardent affection wherewith my heart is fired with the pleasant hopes of your comfortable smiles, I am like to die desperat, and then the 25 world will accuse you of cruelty, in murdering a constant Lady: but if it shall please you to grant me loue, and so espouse me according to Himens holy Rites, heere shall you rule sole King, and be the Lord of all this Countrey.

My right deare Lady (answered then the Red-rose Knight) you haue 30 done such pleasure to mee, and to my distressed followers, in preseruing vs from famine, as I shal neuer requite it, though I should spend all the rest of my life in your Seruice. And know (most excellent Princesse) that there is no aduenture so dangerous, yet at your commandement

25

would I practise to accomplish: yet for to tye my selfe in Wedlockes bonds, there is no woman in the world shall procure mee: for till I haue finished an Aduenture which in my heart I haue vowed, I will not linke my affection to any Lady in the world. But thinke not (Madam) that I refuse your loue through disdaine: for I sweare by the dignity King Arthur grac'd mee with, I should think my selfe most fortunate, if I had so faire and noble a Lady, as your diuine selfe.

Most worthy Knight (then answered the Queene) I imagine, that the Gods haue sent you into this Countrey for two causes principally: The [D₃] first is, that you and your followers/should be preserued from death by my meanes: The second is, that you should inhabit in this Countrey least it should in short time be left as a desert wildernesse: for it is inhabited onely by Women without a King, and haue no other Gouernour but me, which am their chiefe Princesse: And for so much as I haue succoured you, so succour you this desolate Citie, that it may be repeopled with your seed: and in so doing you shall accomplish a vertuous deed, and winne to your names an eternall memory to all ensuing ages.

I confesse (quoth the Red-rose Knight,) that you and your Ladies haue succoured mee and my followers in our great necessitie: and in recompence whereof, wee will imploy all our endeauours to the repeopling againe of this Countrey: But in regard of the secret vow my heart hath made, I will not yeeld my selfe to your desires; for if I should infringe my oath, mine Honour were greatly impaired: And before I would commit that dishonourable fact, I would suffer the greatest torment that mans heart can imagine.

Incontinently, when the loue-sicke Queene heard this answere of the English Knight, and perceiued that he was firme in his purpose, shee tooke leaue of him, and departed for that time: the Red-rose Knight likewise withdrew himselfe into his Chamber, pondring in his minde a thousand imaginations. But shee for her part was so troubled in mind, and so wounded with the Darts of blinde Cupid, that when the mistie darknes of night had couered the earth, shee layd her downe vpon her bed, where betwixt Shame and her Heart, began a terrible Battell. Her Heart was incouraged, that shee should goe and lie with him: but shame began

26

to blush, and withstood that perswasion; by which meanes the battell was great, and indured a long time: but at last the Heart was conquerour, and shame vanquished and put to flight, in such sort, that the faire Queene arose from her bed, and went and layd her downe by her beloued Knight, where hee slept: and being in the bed, shee began fearefully to tremble, 5 for shame still followed her vnlawfull practises: where after her quiuering heart began a little to be qualified, with her trembling hand she awaked him, and after spake in this manner.

My most deare and affectionat friend, though like a carelesse wretch [D3ᵛ] I come vnto thee apparelled with Shame, yet let my true Loue colour this 10 my infamous presumption: for your Princely person, and Kingly demeanours, like Adamants haue drawne my steeled Heart to commit this shamefull acte; yet let not my feruent Affection be requited with Disdaine: and although you will not consent to be my wedded Lord and Husband, yet let me bee thy Loue and secret Friend; that a poore distressed Queene 15 may thinke her selfe happy in an Englishmans loue.

When the noble Knight heard the faire Caelias voyce, and felt her by his side all naked, hee was so sore abashed, that hee wist not what to doe: but yet at last hauing the nature and courage of a man, hee turned to her, vsing many amorous speeches, imbracing and kissing each other in 20 such manner, that faire Caelia was conceiued with Child, and waxe great of a right faire Sonne: of whom she was in processe of time safely deliuered; as you shall heare discoursed of at large in the following History.

But to be short, during the space of foure Monethes, the Fayery 25 Ladyes lay with the English Knights, and many of them were conceiued with their seed in such sort, that the Countrey was afterward repeopled with male Children, and what happened amongst them in the meane season, I will passe ouer for this time: for the dayes and nights (that haue no rest) passe on their wonted course: in which time their Shippe was re- 30 plenished with all necessaries, and the Red-rose Knight summoned together Sir Launcelot and the rest: and being assembled, he sayd vnto them.

My good Friends and Countreymen, you know, that long time we haue soiorned in this Countrey, spending our dayes in idle pastimes, to the reproach of our former glories: now my intent is, within these three dayes to depart this Countrey, therefore let euery man make himselfe in readines: for there is no greater dishonour to aduenturous Knights, then to spend their dayes in Ladyes bosomes.

5   When sir Lancelot and the other English Gentlemen heard the for-
[D4] ward disposition of the Red-rose Knight, they were all/exceeding ioy-full, and answered him; that with great willingnesse they would all be ready at the time appointed.

      But now, when the Fayerie Ladies perceiued the preparations that
10 the English Knights made for their departure, they grew exceeding sor-rowfull, and complained one to another in most grieuous manner: but amongst the rest, the Queene was most displeased, who with a sorrowfull and sad heart came vnto the Red-rose Knight, and in this manner com-playned to him.

15   Alas, alas, my deare Lord, haue yee that tyrannous heart, to with-draw your selfe from me, and to forsake me before you see the fruit of your Noble person, which is nourished with my bloud. Deare Knight, behold with pitie my wombe, the chamber and mansion of your bloud: Oh let that be a meanes to stay you, that my Child (as yet vnborne) be
20 not fatherlesse by your departure. And in speaking these words, shee be-gan to weepe and sigh bitterly, and after to whisper secretly to her selfe in this order.

      Oh you immortall heauens, how may mine eyes behold the departure of my ioy! for being gone, all comfort in the world will forsake me, and
25 all consolation flie from me: and contrariwise, all sorrow will pursue mee, and all misfortune come against me. Oh what a sorrow will it be to my soule, to see thee floting on the dangerous Seas, where euery minute, perils doe arise ready to whelme thee in the bottomlesse Ocean! and be-ing once exempted from my sight, my heart for euermore lie in the bed
30 of tribulation, vnder the couerture of mortall distresse, and betweene the sheetes of eternall bewaylings. Yet if there be no remedy, but that thou wilt needes depart, sweare vnto me, that if euer thou doest accomplish thy pretended voyage, (what it is I know not) that thou wilt returne againe to this Country, to tell mee of thy happy fortunes, and that mine

eyes may once more behold thy louely countenance, which is as delectable to my soule, as the Ioyes of Paradise.

When the Noble English Knight vnderstoode that the Queene condescended to his departure, vpon condition of his returne, to which he solemnly protested, if the Gods gaue him life and good fortune, to per- 5
forme her request: whereby the/Fayrie Queene was somewhat recom- [D4ᵛ]
forted: And hauing great hope in the returne of her deare Loue, shee ceased her lamentations. And now (to abridge the Story) the time came that the valiant English-men should goe a Ship-boord: vpon which day, the Red-rose Knight and his followers, tooke leaue of the noble Queene 10
and her Ladies, thanking them for their kinde entertainements, and so went to the Port of the Sea, where they entred their Ships, and so departed from the Fayrie Land. After this, when Caelia had borne her Babe in her wombe full forty weekes, she was deliuered of a faire Sonne, who came afterward to be called the Fayrie Knight: which for this time 15
wee will not touch, but referre it to the second part of this History.

CHAPTER V.

What happened to the English Knights, *after their departure from the* Fayrie Land.

WITH A PROSPEROUS Winde sayled these English Knights, many 20
a League from the Fayerie Land, to their great content and hearts desire, where eueryrything seemed to Prognosticate their happy Aduentures: so vpon a day when the Sunne shone cleare, and a gentle calme Winde caused the Seas to lye as smooth as Christall Ice, whereby their Ship lay floating on the Waues, not able to remooue: For whilest the Dolphins 25
daunc'd vpon the siluer Streames, and the red gild Fishes leapt about the Shippe, the Red-rose Knight requested Sir Lancelot, to driue away the time with some Courtly Discourse, whereby they might not thinke their Voyage ouer long. Vnto which, the good Sir Lancelot most willingly agreed: And although hee was a Martiall Knight, delighting to heare 30

29

the relentlesse sound of angry Drummes, which thunders threats from a Massaker, yet could hee like an Oratour, as well discourse a Louers History: therefore requesting the Red-rose Knight, and the other/English Gentlemen, to sit downe and listen to the Tale that followeth.

The Pleasant History which Sir Lancelot du Lake, *told to the* Red-ROSE Knight, *being a Ship-boord.*

At that time of the yeare, when the Birds had nipt away the tawny leaues, and Flora with her pleasant Flowers, had enricht the earth, and
10 encloathed with Trees, Hearbs, and Flowers, with Natures Tapistrie, when the golden Sunne with his glistering Beames did glad mens hearts, and euery Leafe as it were, did beare the forme of Loue, by Nature painted vpon it: This blessed time did cause the Grecian Emperour to proclaime a solemne Turnament to bee holden in his Court, which as then was
15 replenished with many worthy and valiant Knights: but his desire chiefe-ly was, to beholde his Princely Sonne Valentine, to try his Valour in the Turnament.

Many were the Ladies that repayred thither, to beholde the worthy Triumphes of this young Prince: amongst which number, came the
20 beautifull Dulcippa, a Mayden which as then wayted vpon the Empresse, being Daughter to a Countrey Gentleman. This Dulcippa, like Apollos Flower, being the fayrest Virgin in that company, had so firmely setled her loue vpon the Emperours sonne, that it was impossible to expell it from her heart. Likewise, his affection was no lesse in feruencie then hers: so
25 that there was a iust equality in their Loues and liking, though a differ-ence in their Birthes and Callings.

This Princely Valentine, (for so was the Emperours Sonne called) entred the Listes in costly Armour most richly wrought with Orient Pearles, his Crest encompassed with Saphire Stones, and in his hand a
30 sturdie Launce. Thus mounted vpon a milk-white Steede, hee vaunted foorth himselfe to try his warlike force: and in prauncing vp and downe, hee many times (thorow his Beuer) stole a view of his fayre Dulcippas

30

face: at which time, there kindled in his Breast two sundry Lampes: the
one was to winne the honour of the / day: the other, to obtaine the loue of [E^v]
his Mistresse. On the other side, Dulcippa did nothing but report the valiant acts of his prowesse and chiualrie, in such sort, that there was no other
talke amongst the Ladies, but of Valentines honourable attempts.   5

No sooner was the Turnaments ended, and this loue begun, but
Dulcippa departed to her lodging, where sighes did serue as bellowes to
kindle Loues fire. Valentine in like manner being wounded to death,
still runneth vp and downe to finde a salue for his stanchlesse thirst: so
seekes Dulcippa to restore her former liberty: for, she being both be-   10
loued, and in loue, knew not the meane to comfort her selfe. Sometime
she did exclaime against her wandring eyes, and wished they had bin
blind when first they gazed vpon the beauty of Princely Valentine: Some
times in visions she beheld his face cheerefull, smiling vpon her countenance: and presently againe, shee thought she saw his martiall hands   15
bathed all in purple blood, scorning her loue and former courtesies.
With that shee started from her dreaming passion, wringing her tender
hands, till flouds of siluer dropping teares trickled downe her face: Her
golden haire that had wont to be bound vp in threeds of gold, hung dan-
gling now about her Iuory necke: the which in most outragious sort she   20
rent and tore, till that her haire which before lookt like burnisht Gold,
were died now in purple and Vermillion bloud. In this strange passion
remained this distressed Lady, till the Golden Sunne had three times
lodged him in the Westerne Seas, and the siluer Moone her shining face
in the Pallace of the Christall Cloudes. At this time a heauy slumber   25
possessed all her senses: for she, whose eyes before in three dayes, and as
many nights, had not shut vp their Closets, was now lockt vp in silent
sleepe, lest her heart ouer burthened with griefe, by some vntimely manner should destroy it selfe.

But now returne wee to the worthy Valentine, who sought not to   30
pine in passion, but to court it with the best, considering with himselfe,
that a faint heart neuer gain'd faire Lady: therfore hee purposed boldly
to discouer his loue to the faire Dulcippa, building vpon a fortunate suc-
cesse, considering that she was but Daughter to a Gentleman, and he a

[E2] Prince borne, so/attiring himselfe in costly Silkes, wearing in his Hatte, an Indian Pearle cut out of Ruby red. On eyther side a golden Arrow thrust through a bleeding Heart; to declare his earnest affection. In this manner went he to his belooued Lady, whom he found in company of oth-
5 er Ladies waighting vpon the Empresse: who taking her by the hand, he led her aside into a Gallery neere adioyning: where he began in this manner to expresse the passion of his loue.

Sacred Dulcippa, (quoth hee) in beauty brighter then glistering Cinthia, when with her beames shee beautifies the vales of Heauen. Thou
10 art that Cinthia, that with thy brightnesse dost light my clowdy thoughtes, which haue many dayes been ouer cast with stormy showers of Loue: Shine with thy beames of mercie on my minde, and let thy light conduct me from the darke and obscure Laberinthe of Loue. If teares could speake, then should my tongue keepe silence: Therefore let my sighes
15 bee messengers of true loue. And though in words I am not able to deliuer the true meaning of my desires: yet let my cause beg pitty at your hands. Other wise your deniall drownes my soule in a bottomlesse Sea of sorrow: One of these two (most beautious Lady), doe I desire: either to giue life with a cheerefull smile, or death with a fatall frowne. Valentine hauing
20 no sooner ended his loues oration, but she with a scarlet countenance, returned him this ioyfull answere.

Most Noble Prince, thy words within my heart, hath knit a gordian knot, which no earthly Wight may vntie: for it is knitte with faithfull Loue, and Teares, distilling from a constant minde. My heart which
25 neuer yet was subiect to any one, doe I freely yeeld vp into thy bosome, where it foreuermore shall rest, till the Fatall sisters cut our liues asunder. And in speaking these words, they kissed each other as the first earnest of their loues. With that the Empresse came thorow the Gallerie, who espying their secret conference, presently nursed in her secret hate, which shee
30 intended to practise against the guiltlesse Lady, thinking it a scandall to her Sonnes birth, to match in mariage with one of so base a parentage:
[E2ᵛ] Therefore purposing to crosse their loues with dis-/mall stratagems, and dryerie Tragedies, shee departed to her Chamber, where she cloked her treacheries vp in silence, and pondred in her heart how she might end

32

their loues, and finish Dulcippas life. In this tragicall imagination remained she all that night, hammering in her head a thousand seuerall
practises. But no sooner was the deawy earth comforted with the hote
beames of Apollos fire, but this thirsting Empresse arose from her carefull
bed, penning herselfe closely within her Chamber, like one that made   5
no conscience for to kill: shee in all hast sent for a Doctor of Phisicke,
not to giue Phisicke to restore health, but poyson for vntimely death: who
being no sooner come into her presence, but presently she lockt her Chamber doore, and with an angry countenance, staring him in the face, shee
breathed this horror into his harmelesse eares.   10

Doctor, thou knowest how oft in secret matters I haue vsed thy helpe,
wherein as yet I neuer saw thy faith falsified: but now amongst the rest,
I am to require thy ayd in an earnest businesse, so secret, which if thou
dost but tell it to the whispering windes, it is sufficient to spread it
through the whole world: whereby my practises may be discouered, and   15
I be made a noted reproach to all hearers.

Madame (quoth the Doctor, whose heart harboured no thought of
bloody deeds) what needs all these circumstances, where dutie doth command my true obedience? desist not therefore gentle Empresse, to make
me priuy to your thoughts: for little did he thinke her minde could har-   20
bour so vile a thought: but hauing coniured most strongly his secresie,
she spake to him as followeth.

Doctor, the loue (nay rather raging lust) which I haue spied of late
betwixt my vnnaturall sonne, and proud Dulcippa, may in short time
(as thou knowest) bring a sudden alteration of our state, considering   25
that he being borne a Prince, and descended from a royall race, should
match in marriage with a base and ignoble Mayden, daughter but to a
meane Gentleman: therefore, if I should suffer this secret loue to goe
forward, and seeke not to preuent it, the Emperour might condemne mee
of falshood, and iudge me an agent in this vnlawfull loue; which to   30
avoyd, I have a practise in my head, and in thy hand it lyes/to procure [E3]
thy Princes happinesse, and Countreys good. Dulcippas father (as thou
knowest) dwels about three miles from my Pallace, vnto whose house
I will this day send Dulcippa, about such businesse as I thinke best, where

33

thou shalt bee appoynted, and none but thou to conduct her thither: where in a thicke and bushy groue which standeth directly in the midway, thou shalt giue her the cup of death, and so rid my heart from suspitious thoughts.

5 This bloody practise being pronounced by the Empresse, caused such a terrour to enter into the Doctors mind, that he trembled foorth this sorrowfull complaint.

Oh you immortall powers of Heauen, you guider of my haplesse fortunes, why haue you thus ordained mee to bee the bloody murderer of a 10 chaste and vertuous Lady, and the true patterne of sobrietie: whose vntimely ouerthrow if I should but once conspire, Dianas Nymphs would turne their wonted Natures, and staine their hands with my accursed blood: Therefore most glorious Empresse, cease your determination, for my heart will not suffer my hand to commit so foule a villany.

15 And wilt not thou doe it then, (replyed the Empresse with a mind fraught with rage and blood?) I doe protest (quoth shee) by Heauens bright maiestie, except thou doest consent to accomplish my intent, thy head shall warrant this my secresie. Stand not on termes, my resolute attempt is cleane impatient of obiections.

20 The Doctor hearing her resolution, and that nothing but Dulcippas death might satisfie her wrath, hee consented to her request (and purposed cunningly to dissemble with the bloody Queene) who beleeued that hee would performe what shee so much desired: so departing out of her chamber, she went to the giltlesse Lady, sending her on this fatall mes- 25 sage: who like to haplesse Bellerophon, was ready to carry an embassage of her own death. But in the meane time, the Doctor harbored in his breast a world of bitter woes, to thinke how vilely this vertuous Lady was betrayed: and considering in his minde, how that he was forced by constraint to performe this tragedy; therefore hee purposed not to giue [E3ᵛ] her a cup of Poyson, but a sleeping/Drinke, to cast her into a traunce, which shee should as a cup of death receiue; as well to try her vertuous Constancie, as to rid himselfe from so haynous a crime.

But now returne wee to Dulcippa, who beeing sped of her Message, went with the Doctor, walking on the way, where all the talke which they had, was of the liberall praise of Prince Valentine; who remayned in Court, little mistrusting what had happened to his beloued Lady: and she likewise ignorant of the hurt that was pretended against her life: but being both alone together in the Wood, where nothing was heard but chirping Birds, which with their voyces seemed to mourne at the Ladyes   5 misfortune. But now the Doctor breaking off their former talke, tooke occasion to speake as followeth.

Man of all other creatures (most vertuous Lady) is most miserable, for Nature hath ordayned to euery Bird a pleasant tune to bemoane their misshapps, the Nightingale doth complaine her Rape and lost Virginitie   10 within the desart Groues: the Swanne doth likewise sing a dolefull heauie tune a while before shee dyes, as though Heauen had inspired her with some foreknowledge of things to come. You Madame, now must sing your Swan-like Song; for the pretty Birds (I see) doe drope their hanging heads and mourne, to thinke that you must die. Maruell not Madame;   15 the angry Queene will haue it so. Accurst am I in being constrayned to bee the bloody instrument of so tyrannous a fact. Accurst am I that haue ordained that cuppe, which must by Poyson, stanche the thirst of the bloody Empresse: and most accursed am I, that cannot withstand the angry Fates, which haue appoynted mee to offer outrage vnto vertue.   20 And in speaking these words, hee deliuered the Cup into the Ladyes hands: who like a Lambe that was led to the slaughter, vsed silence for her excuse. Many times lifted shee vp her eyes toward the sacred Throne of Heauen, as though the Gods had sent downe vengeance vpon her giltlesse Soule, and at last breathed foorth these sorrowfull lamentations.   25

Neuer (quoth shee) shall vertue stoope to Vice. Neuer shall Death affright my soule: nor neuer Poyson quench that lasting loue, which my true heart doth beare to Princely Valen-/tine; whose Spirit (I hope)   [E4] shall meete mee in the ioyfull Fields of Elizium, to call those Ghosts, that dyed for Faithfull loue, to beare mee witnesse of my Faith and Loy-   30 alty: and so taking the Cup, shee said. Come, come, thou most blessed Cup, wherein is contained that happy Drinke, which giues rest to troubled mindes. And thou most blessed Wood, beare witnesse, that I mix this banefull Drinke with Teares distilling from my bleeding heart. These

35

Lips of mine that had woont to kisse Prince Valentine, shall now most
willingly kisse this Ground, that must receiue my Corse. The author of
my death, Ile blesse; for shee honours mee, in that I die for my sweet
Valentines sake. And now Doctor to thee (being the instrument of this
5 my Death) I doe bequeath all earthly happinesse: and here withall, I
drinke to Valentines good fortune: So drinking off the sleeping Potion,
shee was presently cast into a traunce; which shee poore Lady, supposed
death. The Doctor greatly admiring at her vertuous minde, erected her
body against an aged Oake, where he left her sleeping, and with all
10 speede returned to the hatefull Queene, and told her, that he had performed her Maiesties command: who gaue him many thanks, and promised to requite his secrecie with a large recompence.

But now speake we againe of Prince Valentine, who had intelligence,
how the onely comfort of his heart had ended her life by Poysons vio-
15 lence: for which cause, he leaues the Court; and converted his rich
Attire to ruthfull Roabes: his costly coloured Garments, to a homely
russet Coat; and so trauailing to the solitary woods, he vowed to spend
the rest of his dayes in a Shepheards life: His royall Scepter was turned
into a simple Sheepehooke, and all his pleasure was to keepe his Sheepe
20 from the teeth of the rauenous Wolues.

Three times had glistering Phoebe renewed her horned winges, and
deckt the elements with her smiling countenance: Three moneths were
past, three Moones had likewise runne their wonted compasse, before the
Grecian Emperour mist his Princely Sonne: whose want was no sooner
25 bruted through the Court, but hee ecchoed foorth this horrour to himselfe.
[E4ᵛ]   What cursed Planet thus indirectly rules my haplesse course? or
what vncouth dryery Fate hath bereaued me of my Princely sonne? Ioue
send downe thy burning Thunderbolts, and strike them dead that be pro-
curers of his want: But, if (sweet Venus) he be dead for loue, houer his
30 Ghost before mine eyes, that hee may discouer the cause of his afflictions.
But contrariwise, if his life be finished by the fury of some murtherous
mind, then let my exclamations pierce to the iustfull Maiestie of Heauen,
that neuer Sunne may shine vpon his hated head, which is the cause of
my Valentines decay: Or, that the angry Furies may lend me their burn-

ing whips, incessantly to scourge their purple soules, till my Sonnes wrongs bee sufficiently reuenged. Thus, or in such a like frantick humour ranne hee vp and downe his Pallace, till Reason pacified his outragious thoughts, and by perswasion of his Lords, he was brought into his quiet bed. Meanespace, Diana (the Queene of Chastitie) with a Traine of 5 beautifull Nimphes, by chance came through the Wood where Dulcippa was left in her traunce: in which place, rousing the Thickets in pursuit of a wilde Hart, the Queene of Chastity espied the harmlesse Lady stand-ing against a Tree, and beheld her sweet breath to passe through her closed lips: At whose presence, the Queene a while stood wondring at; 10 but at last, with her sacred hand shee awaked her, and withall asked the cause of her traunce, and by what meanes she came thither? Which poore awaked Lady, being amazed both at her sodaine Maiestie, and the strangeness of her passed Fortune and distresse, with farre fetcht sighes, shee related what happened to her in those desart Woods. The heauenly 15 Goddesse being moued with pitie, with a most smiling voyce cheared her vp, and with a Lilly taken from the ground, she wiped the teares from off Dulcippas tender cheekes, which like to a riuer trickled from her Christall eyes. This being done, Diana with an Angels voyce, spake vnto her as followeth. 20

Sweete Virgine (for so it seemeth thou art) farre better would it befit thy happy estate (happy I terme it) hauing past so many dangers, to spend the remnant of thy life amongst my Traine of Nimphes, whereas springeth nothing but Chastity and purity of life. Dulcippa, though in her loue both firme and/constant, yet did she condiscend to dwell with [F] Dianas Nimphs: where now, instead of parly with courtly Gallants, shee singeth Songs, Carrols, Roundelayes: in stead of Penne and Incke, where-with she was wont to write Loue-letters, shee exerciseth her Bow and Arrows, to kill the swift-fat Deare: and her downie Beddes are pleasant Groues, where pretty Lambes doe graze. 30

But now returne wee againe to the raging Emperour, who sifted the matter out in such sort, that hee found the Empresse giltie of her Sonnes want, and the Doctor to bee the instrument of Dulcippas death: who being desperat (like one that vtterly detested the cruelty of the Empresse)

37

would not alleadge, that he had but set the Lady in a traunce, but openly
confessed that he had poysoned her and for that fact was willing to offer
vp his life to satisfie the Law, therefore the angry Emperour sweares, that
nothing shall satisfie his Sonnes reuengement, but death: and thereupon
5 straightly commaunded the Empresse to be put in prison, and the Doctor
likewise to be lockt in a strong Tower: but yet because shee was his law-
full Wife, and a Princesse borne hee something sought to mittigate the
Law, that if anyone within a tweluemonth and a day would come and
offer himselfe to combate in her cause against himselfe, which would be
10 the appealant Champion, she should haue life: if not to bee burnt to ashes,
in sacrifice of his Sonnes death: all which was performed as the Emperour
had commanded.

But now all this while the poore Prince liues alone within the Woods,
making his complaints to the flockes of Sheepe and washing their wooll
15 with his distressed teares. His bedde whereon his body rested, was turned
into a Sun-burnd bank: his chaire of state, couered with grasse: his musicke, the whistling winds: the Rethoricke, pittifull complaints and
moanes, wherewith he bewayled his passed fortunes, and the bitter crosses
of his vnhappy loue:

20 The solitarie place wherein this Prince remained, was not farre
distant from the Groue, where Dullcippa led her sacred life: who by
chaunce in a morning at the Sunnes vprising, attyred in greene vestments,
[Fᵛ] bearing in her hand a/Bow bended, and a quiuer of arrowes hanging at
her backe, with her hayre tyed vp in a Willow wreath, least the Bushes
25 should catch her golden Tresses to beautifie their branches: in this manner comming to hunt a sauage Hart, she was surprized by a bloody Satire
bent to rape, who with a bloody mind pursued her: and comming to the
same place where Prince Valentine fedde his mourning Lambes, hee
ouertooke her, whereat shee gaue such a terrible shrike in the Wood, that
30 shee stird vp the Shepherds princely mind to rescue her: but now when
the bloody Satyre beheld a face of Maiestie shrowded in a shepherds cloth-
ing, immediatly hee scudded through the Woods more swifter then euer
fearefull Deare did run.

But now gentle Reader, heere stay to reade a while, and thinke vpon

38

the happy meeting of these Louers: for surely the imagination thereof will lead a golden witte into the Laberinth of heauenly ioyes: but being breathlesse in auoyding passed dangers, they could not speake a word, but with steadfast eyes stood gazing each other in the face: but comming againe to their former senses Vallentine brake silence with this wauering speach.   5

What heauenly wight art thou (quoth hee) which with thy beautie hast inspired me?

I am no Goddesse (replyed shee againe) but a Virgin vowed to keepe Diana companie, Dulcippa my name: a Lady sometime in the Grecian 10 Court, whilst happy fortune smilde; but being crost in loue, here doe I vow to spend the remnant of my dayes. And with that, hee catching the word out of her mouth, said.

Oh you immortall Gods: and is my Dulcippa yet aliue? I, I, aliue I see she is: I see that sweet celestiall beautie in her face, which hath ban- 15 ished deepe sorrow from my heart: and with that kissing her, hee said. See, see, faire of all faires that Nature euer made, I am thy Valentine, thy vnhappy Loue, the Prince of Greece, the Emperours true Sonne, who for thy louely sake, am thus disguised, and for thy loue, haue left the gallant Court, for this sweet and homely country life. With that, shee tooke him 20 about his manly necke, and breathed many a bitter sigh into his bosome: and after with/weeping teares, discoursed all her passed dangers, as well [F2] the crueltie of the Empresse, as of the vertuous deed of the good Doctor. And hauing both recounted their passed fortunes, they consented (dis- guised as they were) to trauell to the Grecian Court to see if the Destenies 25 had transformed the state of the Emperour or his regiment: for now no longer outcries, nor heauie stratagems, or sorrowfull thoughts sought to pursue them; but smiling fortune, gratious delights, and happy blessings. Now Fortune neuer meant to turne her wheele againe, to crosse them with calamities, but intended with her hand to powre into their hearts 30 oyle of lasting peace. Thus whilst Apolloes beames did parch the tender twigs, these two Louers sate still vnder the branches of a shadie Beech, recounted still their ioyes and pleasures: and sitting both thus vpon a grassy bancke, there came trauelling by them an aged old man: bearing in his withered hand a scaffe to stay his benummed body: whose face when Prince Vallentine beheld, with a gentle voyce he spake vnto him in this sort.

Father, God saue you: How happeneth that you wearied with age, 5 doe trauell through the desart Groues, befitting such as can withstand the checkes of Fortunes ficklenes? Come faire old man sit downe by vs: whose mindes of late were mangled with griefe, and crost with worldly cares.

This good old Hermite hearing the curteous request of the Prince, 10 sate downe by them, and in sitting downe, he fumbled foorth this speech.

I come (young man) from yonder Citie, whereas the Emperour holds a heauy Court, and makes exceeding sorrow for the want of his eldest Sonne, and for a Lady which is likewise absent: the Empresse being found guilty of their wants, is kept close prisoner, and is condemned to bee 15 burnt, vnlesse within a tweluemoneth and a day, she can get a Champion that will enter Battaile in her cause: and with her, a Doctor also is adiudged to suffer death. Great is the sorrow that is there made for this noble Prince, and none but commends his vertue: and withall the deserued praises of the absent Lady.

[F2ᵛ]   Father (replyed then the Prince) thou hast told vs tydings/full of bitter truth, able to enforce an iron heart to lament: for cruell is the doome, and most vnnaturall the Emperour, to deale so hardly with his Queene.

Nay (quoth the old man) if she be guilty, I cannot pitty her, that will 25 cause the ruine of so good a Prince: for higher powers must giue example vnto their subiects.

By Lady Father (quoth the Princely Shepheard) you can well guesse of matters touching Kings; and to be a witnesse of this accident, wee will presently goe vnto the Court and see what shall betide vnto this dis- 30 tressed Queene. This being said, they left the aged man, and so trauailed towards the Grecian Court: and by the way, these Louers did consult, that Prince Valentine attired like a Shepheard, should offer himselfe to combat in his Mothers cause, and so to expresse the kinde loue and nature which was lodged in his Princely breast. But being no sooner arriued in

40

the Court, and seeing his Father to take the combat vpon himselfe, presently he kneeled downe, and like an obedient Sonne, discouered himselfe, and withall Dulcippas strange fortunes: whereupon the Empresse and the Doctor were presently deliuered, and did both most willingly consent to ioyne these two Louers in the bands of Mariage: whereafter they spent 5 their dayes in peace and happinesse.

This pleasant Discourse being ended, which Sir Lancelot had told to the exceeding pleasure of the greatest company, but especially of the Red-rose Knight, who gaue many kind thanks. At this time the windes began to rise, and blow cheerefully, by which they sayled on their iourney suc- 10 cesfully from one coast to another, till at the last they arriued vpon the coasts of Prester Iohns Land, which was in an euening when the day began to loose her christall Mantle, and to giue place to the Sable garments of gloomy night: where they cast Anchor, vnseene of any of that Countreys Inhabitants. 15

CHAPTER VI.

What happened to the Red-ROSE Knight, *and*
his company *in the* Court of Prester Iohn, *and*
how the Red-ROSE Knight *slew a Dragon*
with three tongues, that kept a golden Tree 20
in the same Country: *with other attempts that*
happned.

THE NEXT MORNING by the breake of day, the Red-rose Knight rose from his Cabbin, and went vpon the Hatches of the Shippe, casting his eyes round about, to see if hee could espie some Towne or Cittie where 25 they might take harbour: and in looking about hee espied a great spacious Cittie, in the middle whereof stood a most sumptuous Pallace, hauing many high Towers standing in the ayre like the Grecian Piramides, the which he supposed to be the Pallace of some great Potentate: therefore calling Sir Lancelot (with two other Knights) vnto him, hee requested 30

them to goe vp into the Citie, and to enquire of the Countrey, and who
was the Gouernour thereof; the which thing they promised to doe: so
arming themselues, (as it was conuenient, being strangers in that Country) they went vp into the Citie; where they were presently presented
5 vnto Prester Iohn, who (being alwayes liberall and courteous vnto
Strangers) gaue them a royall intertainment, leading them vp into his
Pallace: and hauing intelligence that they were English-men, and aduenturous trauailours, he sent foure of his Knights for the rest of their
company, desiring them in the Knights behalfe, to returne to the Court,
10 where they should haue a friendly welcome, and a Knightly entertainment.

Thus when the Red-rose Knight had vnderstoode the will of Prester
Iohn, by his foure Knights, the next euening with his whole company hee
repaired to the Cittie, which was right Noble and fayre, and although
15 it was night, yet were the Streetes as light as though it had beene mid-
[F3ᵛ] day, by the cleare/resplendant brightnesse of Torches, Cressetts, and
other Lights which the Citizens ordained to the intertaining of the English Knights. The Streets through which they passed to goe to the Kings
Pallace, were filled with people, as Burgomasters, Knights, and Gentle-
20 men with Ladies and beautifull Damosels, which in comely order stood
beholding their comming. But when the Red-rose Knight was entred
the Pallace: hee found the renowned Prester Iohn sitting vpon his Princely Throne, vnder-propt with pillers of Iasper stone: who after he had
giuen them an honorable welcome, he took the Red-rose Knight by the
25 hand, and led him vp into a large and sumptious Hall, the richest that
euer he had seene in all his life: But in going vp certaine stayres hee
looked in at a window, and espied fayre Anglitora the Kings daughter,
sporting amongst other Ladyes; which was the fayrest mayde that euer
mortall eye behelde, and I thinke that Nature her selfe could not frame
30 her like: but being entred the Hall, they found the Tables couered with
costly fare ready for supper: when as the English Knights were set at
the Kings Table in company of Prester Iohn and Anglitora, with other
Ladyes attending (hauing good stomaches) they fedd lustily; but Anglitora which was placed right ouer against the Red-rose Knight, fedde

42

only vpon his beauty and princely behauiour, not being able to withdraw her eyes from his diuine excellencie: but the renowned Prester Iohn for his part, spent away the supper time, with many pleasant conferences touching the countrey of England and King Arthurs princely Court: the report of which fame, had so often sounded in his eares. But amongst 5 all other deuises, he told the English Knights of a Tree of gold, which now grew in his Realme, and yeerely brought foorth golden fruit, but he could not enioy the benefit thereof, by reason of a cruell Dragon that continually kept it: for the conquest of which golden tree, hee had many times solemnly proclaimed through that part of the World, that if any 10 Knight durst attempt to conquer it, and by good fortune bring the aduenture to an end, he should haue in reward thereof his Daughter the faire Anglitora in marriage: to which many Knights resorted as well of forraine Countreys, as his owne Nation; but none proued so fortunate to/accomplish the wished conquest, but lost their liues in the same aduenture: 15 therefore I fully beleeue, if all the Knights in the world were assembled together, yet were they all vnsufficient to ouercome that terrible Dragon. [F4]

With that the Red-rose Knight with a bold courage stood vp, and protested by the loue he bore vnto his countryes King, he would performe the enterprise, or lose his life in the attempt: so in this resolution hee re- 20 mained all supper time; which being ended, the English Knights were brought into diuers chambers: but amongst the rest, the Red-rose Knight and Sir Launcelot were lodged neere to the fayre Anglitora, for there was nothing betwixt their Chambers, but a little Gallery: into which being come, and no sooner layd in their beds, but the Red-rose Knight 25 began to conferre with Sir Launcelot in this manner.

What thinke you (quoth he) of the enterprize I haue taken in hand? Is it not a deed of honour and reknowne?

Surely (replyed Sir Launcelat) in my iudgement it is an enterprize of death: for euery man in this countrey adiudgeth you ouercome and de- 30 stroyed, if you but once approach the sight of the Dragon, therefore bee aduised, and goe not to this perrilous aduenture, for you can obtain nothing thereby but reproach and death: and doubtlesse they are counted wise that can shun the misuentures, and keepe themselues from danger.

43

But then (quoth the Red-rose Knight) shall I falsifie my promise; and the promise of a noble minde ought still to bee kept: therefore, ere I will infringe the Vow I haue made, I will be deuoured by the terrible Dragon. And in speaking these words they fell asleepe.

5   During which time of their conference, fayre Anglitora stood at their chamber doore and heard all that had passed betwixt them, and was so surprized with the loue of this gentle Red-rose Knight, that by no meanes shee could restrain her affections: and returning to her chamber, casting her selfe vpon her Bedde thinking to haue slept, but could not, 10 shee began to say secretly to her selfe, this sorrowfull lamentation.

    Alas mine Eyes, what torment is this you haue put my heart vnto? for [F4ᵛ] I am not the woman that I was wont to be,/for my heart is fiered with a flame of amorous desires, and is subiect to the Loue of this gallant English Knight, the beautie of the world, and the glory of Christendome. But 15 fond foole that I am, wherefore doe I desire the thing which may not be gotten, for I greatly feare, that hee is already betrothed to a Lady in his owne Countrey. And furthermore his minde is garnished with Princely cogitations, that I may not enioy his Loue: and he thinketh no more of me, then on her that he neuer saw. But graunt that hee did set his affec- 20 tion vpon mee, yet were it to small purpose; for he is resolued to aduenture his life in the conquest of the Golden tree, where hee will soone bee deuowred by the terrible Dragon. Ah, what a griefe and sorrow will it be to my heart, when I shall heare of his vntimely death for hee is the choise of all Nature, the Prince of Nobilitie, and the flowre of worship: 25 for I haue heard him say, that hee had rather die honourably in accomplishing his Vow, then to returne with reproach into England. Which happy country, if these eyes of mine might but once behold, then were my soule possessed with terrestriall ioyes. Anglitora with these words fell asleepe, and so passed the night away till the day came: who no sooner 30 with his bright beames glistered against the Pallace walles, but the Redrose Knight arose from his bed, and armed himselfe in great courage, ready for the aduenture: where after hee had taken leaue of the King, and all the rest of his English friends, hee departed foorth of the Citie towards the Golden tree, which stood in a low vally, some two miles from the Kings Pallace:

This morning was fayre and cleare, and not a cloud was seene in the elements, and the Sun cast his resplendant beames vpon the earth: at which time the Ladyes and Damosels mounted vpon the highest Towers 5 in the Pallace, and the common people came vp to the battlements and walles of Churches, to behold the aduenture of this valiant Knight, who as then went most ioyfully on his iourney, till he came to the vaile of the Golden tree, wherein being no sooner entred, but he behelde a most cruell and terrible Dragon come springing out of his hollow Caue. This Dragon 10 was farre more bigger then a horse; in length full thirtie foote, the which incontinently as soone / as hee was out of his Caue, began to raise his necke, [G] set vp his eares, and to stretch himselfe, opened his throate, and casting foorth thereat most monstrous burning flames of fire: Then the Red-rose Knight drew out his good Sword, and went towards him, whereat the 15 Monster opened his terrible throat, whereout sprang three tongues, casting foorth flaming fire in such sort, that it had almost burnt him. The first blowe that the Knight strooke, hit the Dragon betwixt the two eyes so furiously that hee staggered: but being recouered, and feeling himselfe most grieuously hurt, hee discharged from his throat such abundance of 20 thicke fuming smoake, that it blinded the Knight in such sort, that hee saw nothing: but yet not withstanding hee lifted vp his Sword, and discharged it vpon the Dragon where he imagined his head was, and strooke so furious a blow, that hee cut off his three tongues close by their rootes: by which the Dragon indured such marueilous paine, that hee turned his 25 body so sodainely round, that his tayle smote the valiant Knight a mighty blow vpon his backe, whereby hee fell downe vpon the Sands; being thus ouerthrowne, hee was in minde most marueylously ashamed, but after a while, hauing recouered himselfe, hee ran to the Dragon againe, and with his good Sword smote such a terrible blow vpon his tayle, that it cut 30 it off in the middle: the which peece was seuen foote in length. The Dragon through the great paine that hee felt, came and incountred the Knight in such a fashion that he beate him downe to the ground, and

45

after stood ouer him as though he had been dead: but the Knight tooke his Sword, and vnderneath him thrust it vp to the Hilts so farre that it pierced his heart: which when the Dragon felt as smitten to death, began to runne away with the Sword sticking in his belly, thinking to haue
5 hidden himselfe in his Caue but his life departed before hee could get thither. Incontinently, when the Red-rose Knight had rested himselfe, and saw that the Dragon was dead, he recomforted himselfe, and went and drew out his Sword from his belly, which was all to be-stayned with his blacke blood; and after tooke the Dragons three Tongues and stucke
10 them vpon his Sword; and likewise pulled a branch from the golden
[G^v] Tree, which hee/bore in his hand: and so in triumph went towards the Cittie: and being come within the sight thereof, hee lifted vp the Golden branch into the ayre as high as he could, that it might glister in the Sunne for the people to behold, (which stood vpon high Turrets, expecting his
15 comming,) who perceiuing it, with great admiration began to wonder. Some there were that gathered greene Hearbes and Flowers, and strewed the way whereas the Knight should passe to goe to the Kings Pallace, saying: that all Honour ought to bee giuen to so noble and glorious a Conquerour.

20   Faire Anglitora amongst all other, was most ioyfull, when she beheld the glistering brightnesse of the Golden branch, and commanded her Waighting-maydes to put on their richest attyres, to solemnize the honour of that excellent Victory.

      And to conclude, he was met at the Citie gate, with the mellody of
25 Drummes and Trumpets, and so conducted to the Kings Pallace: where he was right honorably entertayned of Prester Iohn and his Nobles. Surely there is no man so elloquent, that can discourse by writing the great ioy that Anglitora tooke at his returne: and generally the whole Inhabitants had thereat exceeding pleasure.

30   But now when the valiant Red-rose Knight had entered the Hall, and had set the Golden branch vpon an Iuory Cupboard richly furnished with costly Plate, the English Knights and many other Ladyes began to daunce most ioyfully, and to spend the time in delicious sports till Supper was ready, and then the King and the Red-rose Knight was set: and with

them, the noble and faire Anglitora, Launcelat du Lake and other Eng-lish Knights: where (all supper while) there was no other conference holden, but of the valiant encounters of the Red-rose Knight: who for his part did nothing but make secret loue signes to faire Anglitora.

What shall I make long circumstances? The Supper passed, and the 5 houre came that the generall company withdrew them into their Cham-bers, the Red-rose Knight was conducted to his Lodging by many Noble men and others, which brought the Golden branch after him, and so be-queathed him for that night to his silent rest. But presently after the Noble-/mens departure, Anglitora entred into his Chamber, bearing [G2] in her hand a siluer Bason full of warme perfumed Waters, the which shee had prouided to wash the Dragons blood from his body: which when the Red-rose Knight perceiued, and thinking vpon the kind loue that shee proffered him, put off his Cloathes, and made himselfe ready to wash. Faire Anglitora being attired in a white Frocke without sleeues, turned 15 vp her Smocke aboue her elbowes, and so with her owne hands washed the body of the Red-rose Knight.

But now when this gentle Batcheler beheld her louely Body, her faire and round Breasts, the whitenesse of her Flesh, and that hee felt her Hands marueilous soft, hee was so much inflamed with the ardent desire 20 of loue, that in beholding her Beauty, hee began to embrace her, and kissed her many times most courtiously: and so after, when he had been well washed, Anglitora caused him to lie in his Bedde, beholding his well formed limbes, of colour faire and quicke, and could not turne her eyes from his sight: Thus as they were beholding each other without speaking 25 any word, at last the noble Knight spake to her in this manner.

Most deare Lady, you know that by this Conquest, I haue deserued to bee your Husband; and you, through kind loue, to be my Wife; where-by I may say, that you are mine, and I am yours: and of our two Bodies, there is but one: Therefore I require you to seale vp the first quittance of 30 our loues, which is, that wee two for this night, might sleepe together: and so accomplish the great pleasure that I haue so long wished for.

Ah most Noble Knight (answered the faire Lady) what in mee lyeth (that may bring you the least motion of content) shall with all willing-

nesse be performed: But yet I coniure you by the promise of true Knighthood, that you will saue mine Honour, lest I bee made a scandall to my
Fathers glory.

There is no man in the world (quoth he) that shall preserue thine
5 Honour more then I. What if you sleepe this night with me in bed, doe
you any more then your duty, in that I am your Husband, and best beloued Friend.

[G2ᵛ] My deare loue (replyed she againe) there is no pleasure which/I will
deny yee: but for this night, you shall haue patience: for I will neuer
10 yeeld vp the pride of my Virginitie, till my Father hath giuen me in
Mariage: and therefore I desire you, that to morrow you will request
that fauour at his hands: which being graunted and performed, then accomplish your content.

When the Red-rose Knight had vnderstood his Ladyes minde, hee
15 like an Honourable Gentleman, was content to obey her request. What
shall I say more? but that the night drew on to the wonted time of sleepe,
which caused these two Louers (for the time) to breake off company.
Here slept the Red-rose Knight till the next morning: which at the breake
of day, was presented with a Consort of Musicke, which the King him-
20 selfe brought into his Chamber. Their melody so highly contented his
minde, that he threw them a Gold chaine, which was wrapped about his
wrist: a gift plainely expressing the bounty that beautified his princely
breast. The Musicians being departed, hee arose from his rich Bed, and
went vnto the King, whom he found as then walking in a pleasant Gar-
25 den: of whom he required his Daughter Anglitora in marriage, in recom-
pense of his aduenture. The which request so displeased the King, that
all his former curtesies was exchanged into sodaine sorrow, and would
by no meanes consent that Anglitora should bee his betrothed Spouse;
and answered: that first hee would loose his Kingdome, before shee
30 should bee the wife of a wandring knight.

The noble Red-rose Knight, when hee vnderstood the vnkind answere of Prester Iohn (all abashed) went vnto Sir Launcelat, and his
other friends, and certified them of all things that had happened: who
counselled him, that the next morning they should depart.

48

After this conclusion, they went to the King, and thanked him for the high Honour hee had grac'd them with: and, after that, went and visited their Shippe, where for that day they passed the time in pleasure: and so when the scouling night approached, the Red-rose Knight went to the faire Anglitora, and certified her of the vnkind answere of her cruell 5 Father: whereat shee grew sorrowfull, and grieued in minde: but/at [G3] last better considering with her selfe, shee yeelded her fortune fully at his pleasure, promising, that for his loue, shee would forsake both Countrey, Parents, and Friends, and follow him to what place soeuer hee pleased to conduct her. And it is to be supposed, that this night the fayre 10 Anglitora tooke all the richest Iewels which shee had, and trussed them in a fardle, and so when it was a little before day, shee came vnto the Red Rose Knight and awaked him: who presently made him ready, and so departed secretly from his Chamber, till they came to their Shippes: where they found all the rest of the English Knights ready to depart: So, 15 when they were all a Board they hoysted Sayle, and departed from the Port. To whose happy iourney, we will now leaue them for a time, and speake of the discontents of Prester-Iohn, who all that night was exceeding sorrowfull for the vnkind answere, which he had giuen to the Red-Rose Knight, and so Melancholly that he could neither sleepe nor rest: 20 but at the last hee concluded with himselfe, that he would goe and conuey the English Knights (at their departing) vnto their Ships; to the end that being in other countreys, they might applaud his courtesies vsed to Strangers.

So in the morning hee arose and went to the Chamber where the 25 Red rose Knight was lodged, whom hee found departed contrary to his expectation. After that, he went into his Daughters Chamber, where he found nothing but relentlesse walles, which in vaine hee might speake vnto: whose absence droue him into such a desperate minde, that hee suddenly ran to the Sea coastes, where hee found many of his Citizens, 30 that shewed him the Shippes wherein the English Knights were, which was at that time from the Port or Hauen, more then halfe a mile. Then the King (weeping tenderly) demaunded of them, if they had seene his Daughter Anglitora? To whom they answered, that they had seene her

49

vpon the Shippe hatches in company of the Red-rose Knight. At which the King bitterly lamented, beating his Brest, and tearing his milke-white Hayre from his Head, vsing such violence against himselfe, that it greatly grieued the beholders.

[G3ᵛ] At that time there was many of his Lords present, who by/gentle perswasions, withdrew him from the Sea coasts to his Pallace: where he many dayes after, lamented the disobedient flight of his Daughter.

CHAPTER VII.

How Caelia *the* Queene *of the* Fayrie Land *was*
found dead, floting vpon the waues of the
Sea: *with other things that happened to the*
English Knights.

MANY DAYES the windes blew chearfully in such sort, that the English Ships were within kenning of the Fayery Land: at which Sir Lancelat tooke an occasion to speak vnto the Red-rose Knight, and put him in remembrance how hee had promised Caelia to returne into her Countrey: vnto which hee answered, and said: That he would keepe promise, if the Destenies did afford him life. And thereupon commanded the Master Pilot to make thitherward: but the windes not being willing, raysed such a Tempest on the Sea, that the Shippe was cast a contrary way, and the Marriners by no means possible could approach the Fayery land. At which time, the noble Queene Caelia stood by the sea side vpon an high Rocke, beholding the English Ship as it passed by, as her vsual manner was euery day standing, expecting her deare Loues returne, many times making this bitter lamentation to her selfe.

Ah gentle Neptune, thou God of Seas and Windes, where is my desired Loue? bring him againe vnto mee, that day and night weepeth for his company. Thus she complained at the same instant when her Louers Shippe sayled by; for surely she knew it by the Banners and Ensignes which were displayed in the winde: but when the poore Lady perceiued the Ship to turne from her, she was sore abashed and dismayed. In stead of ioy, she was forced to weepe teares: and instead of singing, was constrained to make sorrowfull complaints. In this manner she aboad there all that ensuing night, and caused Fires and/ great Lights to be made on the shore, thinking thereby to call the Red-rose Knight vnto her. 5

This order kept shee euery day and night for the space of sixe weekes, wayling the want of him, whom she loued more deare then her owne heart: but when the sixe weekes were past, and that the Fayerie Queene perceiued that she should have no tydings of her Loue, she went from the Rocke (all in dispaire) into her Chamber; where being entred, shee 10 caused her Sonne to be brought vnto her, whom shee kissed many times, for the loue she bore vnto his Father: and after beholding the little Infant, crossing her Armes, with a sigh comming from the bottome of her heart, she sayd: Alasse my deare Sonne, alasse thou canst not speake to demaund tydings of thy Father, which is the brauest Knight, the most vertuous, 15 and the most valiant in Armes that God euer formed. Oh where is Nature (sweet Babe) that should enioyne thee to weepe, and my selfe more then thee, for the losse of so braue a Prince; whose face I neuer more shall see? Oh cruell and vnkind Fortune: my heart hath concluded, that I goe and cast my selfe, headlong into the Sea, to the intent, that if the Noble Knight 20 bee there buried, that I may lye in the same Sepulchre or Tombe with him: where contrariwise, if hee be not dead, that the same Sea that brought him hither aliue, bring me to him being dead. And to conclude, before I commit this desperate murther vpon my selfe, with my Blood I will write a Letter, which shall bee sewed to my Vestments or Attyre, 25 to the intent that if euer my body bee presented to the Red-rose Knight, that then this bloody Letter may witnesse the true loue that I bore him, to the houre of my death.

Many Ladyes and Damsels were in her company whilst thus shee lamented her Knights absence: who hearing of her desperate intended 30 death, made exceeding sorrow. Some there were that so mightily grieued, that they could not speake one word: other some there were that sought to perswade her from her desperate intent: but all in vaine. For she presently went from them, and with her owne blood writ a Letter, and

51

wrapped it in a Sear-cloth, and then sowed it to the Vestures wherein she
[G4ᵛ] was clothed: then taking her Crowne, shee bound it/ from her head with
a Golden chaine which the Red-rose Knight before time had giuen her.
Then when shee had done all this, shee came to her little Sonne, and
5 many times kissed him, and so deliuered him to the Ladyes and Damsels
to bee nourished: and so after taking leaue of them all, she departed
toward the sea, whither being come, she went to the top of the high rock,
where she began to looke downe vpon the Sea, and after casting her selfe
vpon the Earth, looking vp towards Heauen, she sayd.
10   Thou God of my Fortunes, Lord of the Windes and Seas: thou that
broughtest into this country the right perfect Knight, in beauty, manhood, and all vertues, graunt that when my soule hath made passage out
of this world, my body may be intombed in his boosome: which words
being sayd, shee turned her eyes towards her Pallace, and spake with a
15 high voyce: Adue my deare Babe, adue you glistring Towres, my royall
Pallace: adue Ladyes and Damsels: and lastly, adue to all the world,
And in saying so, she cast herselfe into the Sea, and there desperately
drowned herselfe.
   But yet such was her fortune, that the waues of the Sea bore her dead
20 body the same day to the English Knights Ship, which as then lay in a
Road where they had cast Anchor for to rest that night, and to be short,
it so happened at the same houre when her dead Body was cast against
the Shippe, the Red-rose Knight went vp the Hatches to take the fresh
ayre: where (looking about) he espyed the dead Lady richly attyred in
25 cloth of Gold, that gorgiously shone in the Water, the which he presently
caused to be taken vp and brought into the Ship: where looking wishly
vpon her, he knew her perfectly well: and after stooping to kisse her
pale Lippes, hee found the bloudy Letter which she had compiled, wrapt
in Seare-cloth: so, taking it and reading the contents thereof, his Blood
30 began to change, and to wax redde like the Rose, and presently againe
as pale as ashes. Whereat Sir Launcelat and the other Knights were
greatly abashed, but especially Anglitora, who demaunded the cause of
his griefe? Whereunto the Red-rose Knight was not able to answere a
word, the sorrow of his heart so exceeded: yet not withstanding, he de-

52

liuered the bloody letter to Anglitora, the contents whereof are these that follow.

The bloody Letter of Queene Caelia.

Thou bright Star of Europe, thou Chosen of England for prowesse and beautie: When wilt thou return to fulfill thy promise made vnto her,   5
that many a day hath had her eyes planted vpon the Seas after thee, shedding more teares in thy absence, then the Heauens containeth Starres? Ah my deare Loue, makest thou no reckoning nor account of thy promise that thou madest to me at thy departure? knowest thou not, that euery noble mind is bound to keepe his word, vpon paine of reproach and shame?   10
but thou hast infringed it, and hast broken thy oath of Knighthood: which no excuse can recouer. For since I last saw thy Shippe floating on the Seas, I neuer came within my Pallace till the writing hereof, nor neuer lay in Bedde to take my rest, nor neuer sate in iudgement on my Countries causes: but for the space of fortie dayes, I stood vpon a Rocke,   15
expecting thy returne, till famine constrayned me to depart. There haue I stood day and night, in raine and in snow, in the cold of the morning, and in the heate of the Sunne; in fasting, in prayers, in desires, in hope; and finally, languishing in dispaire and death: Where, when I could heare no newes of thy returne, I desperately cast my selfe into the Sea,   20
desiring the Gods, that they would bring mee either aliue, or dead to thy presence, to expresse the true affection that I haue euer borne thy noble Person: Thus fare thou well. From her that liued and dyed with an vnspotted minde.

Thine owne true Louer, till we meete in   25
the Elizian fields: thy vnhappy Caelia
Queene of the Fayerie Land.

Thus when faire Anglitora had read those bloody lines, she greatly lamented her vnhappy death: and withall, requested the Red-rose Knight, in that she dyed for his sake, to beare her Body into England, and there   30
most honourably intombe it: to which he most willingly consented. So

causing her body to be inbalmed, they hoysted sayle, and departed towards England: into which Country, they within foure moneths safely ariued. At whose comming, the Inhabitants and dwellers, greatly reioyced, but chiefely the Red-rose Knight and his company, who at their first ariuall,

5 kneeled downe vpon the Earth, and gaue God thankes for preseruing them from so many dangers and perils, to their high renowne, and triumphant victoryes.

After this, they intombed the body of Caelia most honourably as befitted a Princesse of her calling. This being done, they departed to-

10 wards Pendragon Castle, standing in Walles, where as then King Arthur kept his royall Court: where being ariued, they found the King, and many other Nobles in a readines to giue them a Princely welcome: amongst whom was faire Angellica the Nun of Lincolne, mother to the Red-rose Knight; yet kept in so secret a manner, that neither he, nor she,

15 had any suspition thereof, but spake one to another as meere strangers: The discouery of whom, discoursed at large in the second part of this Historie: as likewise the strange fortune of Caelias little Sonne, which the Ladyes in the Fayerieland called by the name of the Fayerie Knight; and by what meanes he came to be called the Worlds Tryumph: with

20 many other strang accidents, etc. But now (to conclude this first part) the Red-rose Knight and the faire Anglitora were solemnely maried together and liued long time in King Arthurs Court in great ioy, and tranquilitie, and peace.

FINIS.

25   R. I.

54

To the Reader.

ROMISE IS DEBT, (gentle Reader) I haue therefore performed what in my first Part I promised; which was, to shew thee the vnfortunate death of the *Red rose Knight*, his beloued Lady 5 *Anglitoras* disloyal affections towards him, his Childrens Honours, Renownes, and Dignities: and in the period of this small Historie, his death both iustly, truely, and strangely reuenged: The reading of which (if with good consideration) I doubt not but shall bring vnto thee much pleasure and delight, being 10 (for the quantitie thereof) nothing inferiour to the best that hath beene written of the like Subiect (I meane) of Knights aduentures, and Ladyes beloued. I therefore dedicate this to thy reason, knowing that this old Prouerbe may confirme my expectation, which is; That good Wine needs no Bush: nor a pleasing Historie craues no shelter. Farewell. 15

R. J.

55

THE
Second Part of the

Famous Historie of Tom a Lincolne, the Red-rose Knight.

Wherein is declared his vnfortunate
Death, his Ladyes disloyalty, his Chil-
drens Honours, and lastly, his Death
most strangely reuenged.

Written by the first Author.

At *London* Printed by *Augustine Matthewes,*
dwelling in the Parsonage House of *Saint*
Brides in Fleete-street. 1 6 3 1.

The Second Part of [H4]

The Famous History of

TOM A LINCOLNE,

the Red-ROSE Knight, &c.

CHAPTER 1   5

How Tom a Lincolne *knew not his* Mother, *till forty yeares of his age, nor whose* Sonne *he was*: Of King Arthurs *death, and his dying speeches, and of what hapned thereupon.*

HEN ARTHUR, that renowned King of Eng- 10
land (being one of the nine Worthies of the
World) had by twelue seuerall set Battailes, conquered the third part of the Earth; and being wearied with the exploytes of Martiall aduentures, in
his olde dayes betooke himselfe to a quiet course of 15
life; turning his Warlike habiliaments, to diuine Bookes of celestiall
meditations: that as the one had made him famous in this World, so
might the other make him blessed in the World to come. Seauen yeares
continued quiet thoughts in his breast: seauen yeares neuer heard he the
sound of delightfull Drums; nor in seuen yeares beheld hee his thrice 20

59

worthy Knights of the Round Table, flourishing in his Court: by which meanes his Pallace grew disfurnished of those Martiall troupes, that drew commendations from all forraigne kingdomes. In this time, most of those renowned Champions, had yeelded their liues to the conquering Tiranny
5 of pale Death, and in the bowels of the Earth lay sleeping their eternall
[H4ᵛ] sleepes, the royall/King himselfe laden with the honour of many yeeres; and hauing now (according to nature) the burthen of death lying heauie vpon his shoulders: and the stroke lifted vp to diuide his body from his soule, he called before him all the chiefest of his Court: but especially his
10 own Queene, the Red-rose Knight, and his Lady Anglitora, with the faire Angellica, the Nunne of Lincolne, whom hee had so many yeeres secretly loued: and being at the poynt to bid a wofull farewell to the world, with countenance as Maiestical as King Priam of Troy, he spake as followeth.

15   First, to thee my loued Queene, must I vtter the secrets of my very soule, and what wanton escapes I haue made from my nuptiall Bedde, otherwise cannot this my labouring life, depart from my fading body in quiet: Long haue I liued in the delightfull sinne of Adulterie, and polluted our mariage Bed with that vile pleasure: pardon I beseech thee and with that
20 forgiuenesse (which I hope will proceed from thy gentle heart) wash away this long bred euill, the Celestiall powers haue graunted me remission. Then turning to Angellica the Nunne of Lincolne, hee said.

    Oh thou my youths delight: thou whose loue hath bereaued my Queene of much mariage pleasure: thou, and but onely thou, haue I
25 offended withall, therefore diuine Angellica, forgiue me: I like a rauisher spotted thy Virginitie. I cropt thy sweet budde of Chastitie; I with flattery won thy heart, and ledde thee from thy Fathers house (that good Earle of London) to feede my wanton desires: by thee had I a Sonne, of whom both thou and I, take glory of: for in his worthynesse remaine
30 the true Image of a Martialist; and this renowned Knight of the Redrose, is he: He liues: the fruit of our wanton pleasures, born at Lincolne, and there by a Shepherd brought vp, few knowing (till now) his true Parents. Maruaile not deere Sonne: thinke not amisse Sweete Queene: nor thou my louely Angellica: Be not dismayde you honourable States,

60

heere attending my dying houre: for as I hope presently to enter into Elizium Paradise, and weare the Crowne of disertfull Glory, I haue re-uealed the long secrets of my heart, and truely brought to light those things, that the/darknesse of obliuion hath couered. Now the Mother [1] knowes her Sonne, the Sonne the Mother. Now may this valiant Knight 5 boast of his Pedegree, and a quiet content satisfie all your doubts. Thus haue I spoke my minde, and thus quieted, my soule bids the world farwell. Adue faire Queene, adue deere son, farwell louely Angellica; Lords and Ladyes adue vnto you all: you haue seene my life, so now behold my death: as Kings doe liue, so Kings must die. These were the last of King 10 Arthurs words: And being dead, his death not halfe so amazed the standers by, as the strange speeches at his liues farwell.

The Queene in a raging ielousie fretted at her Marriage wrongs, protesting in heart, to be reuenged vpon the Nunne of Lincolne.

The Nunne of Lincolne, seeing her wantonnesse discouered, tooke 15 more griefe thereat, then ioy in the finding of her long lost Son; suppos-ing now, that (the King being gone) she should be made a scandall to the world.

The Red-rose Knight, knowing himselfe to be begot in wantonnesse, and borne a Bastard, tooke small ioy in the knowledge of his Mother. 20

Anglitora (Tom a Lincolnes Wife) exceeded all the rest in sorrow, bitterly sobbing to her selfe, and in heart making great lamentation, in that she had forsaken Father, Mother, Friends, Acquaintance, and Coun-trey, all for the loue of a Bastard, bred in the wombe of a shamelesse Strumpet: therefore she purposed to giue him the slip; and with her owne 25 Sonne (a young gallant Knight, named the Blacke Knight, in courage like his Father) to trauaile towards the Kingdome of Prester Iohn, where she first breathed life, and her Father reigned.

In this melancholy humour spent they many dayes, troubling their braines with diuers imaginations. The Court, which before rung with 30 Delights, and flourished in gallant sort, now thundred with Complaints; euery one disliking his owne estate: Discontent as a proud Commaunder gouerned ouer them, and their Attendants were idle Fancies, and disquiet Thoughts: and to speake troth, such a confused Court was seldome seene

61

in the Land; for no sooner was Kinge Arthurs Funerall solemnized, but [I^v] the whole troupes/ of Lords, Knights and Gentlemen, Ladyes, and others, were (like to a splitted Shippe torne by the Tempest of the Sea) seuered, euery one departed whither his Fancie best pleased.

5   The Red-rose Knight conducted his Mother Angellica to a Cloyster in Lincolne, which place she had so often polluted with her shame, there to spend the remnant of her life in repentance; and with her true Lamentations, to wash away her blacke spottes of sinne, that so grieuously stayneth her Soule: and from a pure Virgine, made her selfe a desolute 10 Strumpet.

    Likewise, King Arthurs widdowed Queene, like to irefull Hecuba, or the iealous Iuno, kept her Chamber for many dayes, pondering in her minde what reuenge shee might take vpon Angellica her Husbands late fauorite.

15   On the other side Anglitora Lady and Wife to the Red-rose Knight, with her Sonne the Blacke Knight, made prouision for their departure towards the Land of Prester Iohn, where shee was borne: so vpon a night when neither Moone nor Star-light appeared, they secretly departed the Court, onely attended on by a Negar or Black-more; a Slaue fitting to 20 prouide them necessaries, and to carry their Apparell and Jewels after them; whereof they had aboundant store: The Blacke Knight her Sonne, (so called rather by fierce courage, then his blacke complexion) was all fiered with the ardent desire that hee had to see his Graundsire Prester Iohn: therefore without taking leaue of his Father (being then absent 25 in the company of his leawde Graunde mother) with a noble spirit conducted his mother to the Sea side, where a shippe was ready then to hoyst Sayle, where of the Pilots they were most willingly receiued for Passengers. And in this manner departed they the Land, the Blacke Knight wore on his Helmet for a Scutchon, a blacke Rauen feeding on dead 30 mens flesh; his Caparisons were all of blacke veluet imbrodered, which most liuely figured foorth the blacke furie lodged in his Princely boosome. Anglitora his Mother, had the attyre of an Amazon, made all of the best Arabian silke, coloured like the changeable hue of the Raine-bow: about her necke hung a Jewell of a wounderfull value, which was a Diamond

cut in the fashon of a Heart split asunder with a Tur-/kish Semiter: [I2]
betokening a doubt that shee had of her Knights loyaltie. The Slauish
Moore that attended them, went all naked, except a shaddow of greene
Taffata which couered his priuie parts: vpon his foote a Morischo Shoe,
which is nothing but a Soale made of an Asses hide, buckled with small   5
Leathers to his insteps; vpon his Head hee wore a Wreath of Cypres
guilded with pure gold, and a Plate of Brasse about his necke close locked,
with the word bond-slaue ingrauen about it. In this manner passed they
the Seas, and was by these strange habites wondred at in all Countries
where they came: In which trauels wee will leaue them for a time, and   10
speake of other things pertinent to our story.

CHAPTER 2

Of Tom a Lincolnes *strang manner of trauelling, his wofull departure from* England, *and
of his sorrowfull lamentations for the vn-*   15
kindnesse of his Lady.

WHEN TOM A LINCOLNE (the Red-rose Knight) had spent some
two months in the company of his Mother at Lincolne, giuing her as
much comfort as a Sonne might, hee left her very penitent for her liues
amisse, and returned to the Court, where hee left both his Wife and her   20
Sonne, the Blacke Knight, thinking at his ariuall, to finde so ioyfull a
welcome, and so courtious an intertainement, that all the blacke cloudes
of Discontent might bee blowne ouer by their happy meeting: but as ill
chaunce had allotted all things fell out contrary to his expectation; for
hee neither found Wife, Childe, Seruant, nor any one to make him an-   25
swere: His Plate and Treasure was deminished, his house-hold Furniture, imbesselled, and by Theeues violently carryed away, hee had not
so much as one Steed left in his Stable, for them the Queene had seazed
on for her vse: and furthermore (by her commandement) a Decree was
made, that/ whomsoeuer in all the Land shewed him any duty, or gaue [I2v]

63

him but homely reuerence, should loose their heads, for shee had intitled him, The base borne seed of Lust, a Strumpets brat, and the common shame of the dead King. This was the malice of King Arthurs widow: and assuredly Queene Iuno neuer thirsted more for the confusion of Hercules then shee did for Tom a Lincolns ouerthrow: But yet this griefe (being cast from a Princesse fauour, to a vulgar disgrace) was but a pleasure, to the sorrow he tooke for the misse of his Lady and Sonne: No newes could hee heare of them, but that they were fled from the furie of the angry Queene: which was but a vaine imagination laid vpon the enuious time: but farre otherwise did mischiefe set in her foote, as the doting minde of his Lady Anglitora intended to a further reach, which was to abandon his presence foreuer, and to thinke him as ominous to her sight, as the killing Cockatrice. The effect of this his Wiues sodaine dislike, shee had caused (before her departure) to be carued in stone ouer the Chimny of his lodging, how that She deserued damnation to leaue Father, Friends, and Countrie, for the disloyall loue of a Bastard.

Of all griefes to him this was the very spring, the roote, the deapth, the hight: which when hee had read, hee fell into a sounde, and had it not beene for two Pages that attended him, he had neuer recouered: in this agony the vaines of his breast sprung out into blood, and all the partes of his body sweat with griefe: downe fell hee then vpon his knees, and immediatly pulled the Ring from his finger which shee had giuen him when they were first bethrothed, and wash't it with his teares, kissing it a hundred times: All that euer hee had from her did hee wash in the blood that trickled from his boosome and after bound them in a Cypresse to his left side, directly where his heart lay, protesting by that God that created him, and was the guide of all his passed fortunes, neuer to take them thence, till either hee found his Lady, or ended his life. He likewise made a solemne vow to Heauen, neuer to cut his Haire, neuer to come in Bedde, neuer to weare Sho, neuer to taste Food, but onely Bread and Water, nor neuer to take pleasure in humanitie, till he had eased his griefe in the/ presence of his deerest Anglitora, and that her loue were reconciled to him.

Being thus strangely resolued, hee discharged his Seruants and Pages,

64

giuing them all the wealth that he had, and clad himselfe in tand sheeps skins, made close vnto his Body, whereby hee seemed rather a naked Wilde man bredde in the Wildernesse, then a sencible creature brought vp by ciuill conuersation. Thus bare footed, and bare legged, with an Iuory Staffe in his hand, hee set forward to seeke his vnkind Wife, and 5 vnnaturall Sonne: giuing this wofull farewell to his natiue Countrey.

Oh you celestiall Powers (quoth he) wherefore am I punished for my Parents offences? Why is their secret sinnes, made my publike miserie? What haue I mis-done, that my Wife resisteth me, and like a discourteous Lady forsakes mee, making her absence my present calamitie. 10

Oh thou gratious Queene of Loue, I haue beene as loyall a seruant in thy pleasures, as euer was Hero to her Leander, or Pyramus to his Thisbie: Then what madding furie, like a cruell commander, hath taken possession of my Anglitoras heart, and placed infernall conditions, whereas the pure vertues of modest behauiour had wont to bee harboured? 15 It cannot bee otherwise, but the enraged Queene with her vnquenchable Enuie, hath driuen her hence; and not only of one heart made two, but of two seekes to make none; which is, by vntimely death, to work both our confusions: therefore proud Queene, farewell: let all the furies haunt thee, and may thy Court seeme as hatefull to thy sight, as the torments 20 of Hell fire to a guilty Conscience. Vngratefull England likewise adue to thee, for all the honours I haue brought into thy bounds, and with the spoyles of forraigne Countries, made thee the onely Prince of Kingdomes: yet thou repayest me with disgrace, and load'st mee with more contempt, then my neuer conquered Heart can indure: so kissing the ground with 25 his warme lippes, that had so long fostered him, and with many a bitter teare, and deepe sobbe, like a Pilgrime, (as I said before) hee tooke leaue of his natiue Countrey, and so went to the Sea side; where hee heard of his/Wife and his Sonnes departure, after whom (as soone as the Wind [I3ᵛ] conueniently serued) hee tooke shipbord: Where wee will now likewise 30 leaue him to his fortune vpon the Sea, and speake of the professed malice the Queene prosecuted against Angellica, the mother of the Red-rose Knight.

65

CHAPTER 3

Of *the wofull death of* Angellica, Mother *to the* Red-ROSE Knight, *and of the death of the* iealous Queene *and others.*

5 THE BEAUTIOUS ANGELLICA, beeing left by her Sonne, the Red-rose Knight, (at his departure) in a Monestarie at Lincolne, there to bewaile her former offences; and for her youths pleasure, in age to taste the bitter food of sorrow: the day time shee spent in grieued passions, the night shee wasted with sighs and heartbreaking sobbes: shee fed on

10 carefull thoughts, her drinke was streames of salt teares: her companions, thoughts of her passed wanton pleasures: her bed no better then the cold earth: her sleepes were few, but her comforts lesse: her continuall exercise, was with a Needle to worke in silke vpon the Hangings of her Chamber, how shee was first wooed, then won to King Arthurs pleasures, in what

15 manner their meetings were, their wanton daliances, his imbraces, her smiles: his Princely gifts, her courteous acceptance: and lastly, the birth of her thrice worthy Sonne, his bringing vp, his honours in the Court, and his strange discouerie: all which shee had wrought, as an Arras worke, with silke of diuers collours, in a peece of the purest Holland

20 cloath. In doing this, twise had the golden Sunne runne his circumference about the world, twise had the pleasant Spring beautified the Earth with her changable mantles, twise had nipping Winter made the Fields barren, and the Woods leafelesse: and twise had the yeere shewed himselfe
[14] to all mankind: in which time of/twise twelue moneths, euery day made

25 shee a sorrowfull complaint for the wracke of Honour, and her Virginities losse, which so willingly she surrendred: in this time, so greatly had sorrow and griefe changed her, that her eyes (which had wont like twinckling Diamonds to giue light to all affections) were now sunke into their Cels, and seemed like a hollow Sepulcher new opened: her

30 Face, wherein Beautie her selfe dwelt, and her Cheekes the true die of the Lillie and the Rose intermixt, now appeared old and writhen, like

to the countenance of Hecuba when her husband King Priamus, and all her Princely Children were slaine at Troyes destruction: and her tresses of Gold-like Hayre, which like to Indian Wyers hung ouer her shoulders, were now growne more white then Thistle downe, the Isickles of frozen Ice, or the white mountaine Snow: all these griefes of Nature had not age 5 changed, but the inward griefe of her carefull heart.

But now marke the wofull chance that hapned, euen vpon the day, which by computation she had in former times yeelded vp her Maydens pride, and lost that Iewell that Kingdomes cannot recouer: vpon that haplesse day, came there a Messenger from the Queene, to bid her make 10 preparation for death; for on that day should bee her liues end, and her fortunes period: which she most willingly accepted of, and tooke more ioy thereat, then to be inuited to a Princely Banquet.

Be not dismayde (said the Messenger) for you shall haue as honour-able a death as euer had Lady: seauen seuerall Instruments of death shall 15 be presented to you for a choyse, and your owne tongue shall giue sen-tence which of them you will die by: whereupon this Messenger set this sorrowfull Lady at a round Table, directly in the middle of a very large roome, (whereinto he had led her) hung all about with blacke; where being placed as to a Banquet, or some solemne Dinner of State, there 20 entred seauen Seruitours in disguised shapes like vnto Murtherers, with seauen seuerall deadly seruices in Dishes of siluer Plate: The first, brought in Fire burning in a Dish, if shee would, to consume her body to ashes: The second brought in a Dish, a twisted Coard, to strangle her to death: The third, a Dish full of deadly Poyson, to burst her body 25 withall: The/fourth, a sharpe edg'd Rayzor or Knife, to cut her throat: [I4ᵛ] The fifth, an Iron wracke to teare her body into small peeces: The sixth, a Dish full of liue Snakes, to sting her to death: And the seuenth an im-poysoned Garment, being worne, that will consume both flesh and blood. These seauen deathfull Seruitours hauing set downe their Dishes (the 30 least whereof brings present death) shee was commanded by the Mes-senger, which of them she should choose to die withall, and to make speedy choyce; for he was sworne to the Queene (on whom he attended) to see it that day accomplished. At these his words, shee fell presently vpon her knees, and with a courage readier to yeeld to deaths furie, then to the mercie of the liuing Queene, said as followeth.

Oh thou guider of this earthly Globe, thou that gauest my weake
5 nature ouer to a wanton life, and from a Virgin chast, hast made me an infamous Strumpet: thou that sufferedst only a King in Maiestie to pre-uaile against mee, and with the power of greatnesse wonne mee to lewd-nesse; for which I am now doomed to a present death, and forced by violence, to bidde this tempted world adue; Inspire mee with that happy
10 choyce of death, as my Soule may haue an easie passage from my body. First, to dye by Fire, to an earthly imagination seemes terrible, and farre different from nature: secondly, to die with strangling cord, were base, and more fitting for robbers, theeues, and malefactors: thirdly, to die by deadly poyson, were a death for Beasts and wormes, that feede vpon the
15 bosome of the Earth: fourthly, to die by cutting kniues and slicing razors, were a death for cattle, fowles, and fishes that dies for the vse of man: fiftly by an iron wracke to end my life, were a barbarous death, and against mans nature: but seuenthly, to die a lingring death, which is a life consuming by wearing of impoysoned garments, (where repentance may
20 still bee in company) will I choose: therefore sweet Messenger of my death doe thy office, attyre me in these robes; and the manner of my death I beseech thee make knowne vnto the Queene: tell her (I pray thee) I forgiue her; and may my death bee a quiet vnto her soule, for my life is to her eares as the fatall sound of night Rauens, or the Mer-
25 maides tunes./

[K]   Vaine world, now must I leaue thy flattering intisements, and instead of thy pompe and glory, must shortly treade the dolefull march of pale death: and this body that hath beene so pleasing to a Princes eye, must bee surrendred vp for wormes to feed vpon. Many other words would
30 she haue spoken, but that the commaunding Messenger (being tyed to an houre) caused her to put on the impoysoned Roabes which no sooner came to the warmth of her body, but the good Lady after a few bitter sighes, and dreadfull gaspes yeelded vp the ghost, being (through the ex-tremitie of the infectious Garment) made like vnto an Anatomie; which

68

they wrapped in Seare cloth, and the next day gaue her buriall according to her estate and so returned to the inraged Queene, keeping then her Court at Pendragon castle in Wales, into whose presence was no sooner the Messenger come, but the angry Queene beyond all measure being desirous to heare of Lady Angellicas death, in a rage ran and clasped   5 him about the middle, saying.

Speake Messenger speake, is the vile strumpet dead? Is the shame of womankind tortured? Is my hearts griefe by her death banished my bosome? speake for I am ouermaistred with doubts.

Most gracious Queene (quoth the Messenger) resolue your selfe of   10 her death, for the cold earth hath inclosed vp her body: but so patiently tooke shee her death, that well might it haue mooued a Tygers heart to remorse; for in troth, my heart relented at the manner of her death. Neuer went Lambe more gently to the slaughter, nor neuer Turtledoue was more meeke, then this wofull Lady was at the message of her death: 15 for the Elements did seeme to mourne, closing their bright beauties vp to blacke and sable Curtaines; and the very flintie walles (as it were) sweate at the agonie of her death, so gentle, meeke and humbly tooke shee her death; commending her selfe vnto your maiestie, wishing that her death, might be your soules contentment.   20

And could shee bee so patient (quoth the Queene) that euen in death would wish happinesse to the causers thereof? farewell thou miracle of womankind, I haue been to thee a sa-/uage Lionnesse: I was blinded at [Kᵛ] the report of thy wantonnesse, else hadst thou been now aliue: all my cruelnesse against thee, I now deeply repent, and for thy deare hearts   25 blood by me so rashly spilt, shall bee satisfied with the liues of many soules. Hereupon, shee in a furie commanded the Messengers head to be stricken off, and the seauen Seruitours to bee hanged all at the Court Gate, and afterward caused their limbes to be set vpon high Pooles by the Common high wayes side, as an example of her indignation.   30

Neuer after this houre (such is the remorse of a guiltie conscience) could shee sleepe in quiet, but strange visions of this Lady (as shee thought) seemed to appeare to her: the least noise that she heard whisper- ing in the silence of the night, did she imagine to bee some Furie to

69

dragge her to Hell, for the death of this good Lady: the Windes (as shee imagined) murmured foorth Reuenge, the running Riuers hummed foorth Reuenge, the flying Fowles of the Ayre whistled out Reuenge: yea euery thing that made noyse (in her conceit) gaue remorse for Re-
5 uenge: and till that her owne life had giuen satisfaction by death for the ruine of so sweet a Ladyes life, no food could doe her good, no sleepe quiet her braine, no pleasure content her minde, but Despaire with a terrible countenance, did euermore attend her, willing her sometime to throwe her selfe head-long from the top of a Tower, sometime by poyson to end
10 her dayes, sometime by drowning, sometime by hanging, sometime by one thing, sometime by another: but at last in the middle of the night, hauing her heart deeply ouermaistred by dispaire, shee tooke a Girdle of pure Arabian Silke, which Girdle shee first wore on her Princely Nup-tiall day when King Arthur marryed her: this fatall Girdle shee made a
15 riding knot of, and therewithall vpon her Bed post shee hanged her selfe. Thus blood (you see) being guiltlesse shed, is quitted againe with blood.

The Queene being dead, was not so much pittied of the people, as the good Lady Angellica, little lamentation was made for her death; for euery one expected the like vntimely ende: but according to the aleadge-
20 ance of Subiects her Noblemen gaue her a Princely Funerall, and set ouer
[K2] her an / Iron Tombe, in signification that shee had an Iron heart, and Flintie conditions.

Heere will wee leaue the dead to their quiet restes, and returne to the Blacke Knight, and his Mother Anglitora, with the Indian slaue that at-
25 tends them: for strange bee the accidents that happen to them in forraigne Countryes: and after, wee will speake what hapned to the Red-rose Knight on the Sea.

70

CHAPTER 4

By what meanes Anglitora *became a* Curtizan,
and how her Sonne *the* Blacke Knight *lost
himselfe in a wildernesse.*

THE BLACKE KNIGHT, his Mother Anglitora, and the Blacke-   5
amoor slaue, hauing happily crost the Seas, had ariued in a Countrey
very fertill to see to, replenished with all kinde of Trees and Fruit, yet
were there no Inhabitants to finde, but onely an old Castle built of Flint
stones, the Turrets whereof were made like the Grecian Piramedes,
square and very high: At this Castle gate they knocked so boldly (each   10
one carelesse of all accidents that might happen) as it rung into the
Chamber where the Knight of the Castle lay: who immediatly sent a
very low statur'd Dwarffe to see who knocked, and if they were strangers,
to direct them vp into his Chamber to take such kinde courtesies as the
Castle afforded: for indeed hee was a Knight of a bountifull condition,   15
and full of liberalitie. The Dwarffe no sooner comming to the Gate,
and espying people in such strange disguised attyres, neuer hauing seene
the like before, without speaking one word, ran amazedly vp to his Master, certifiing him, that a kinde of people of an vnknowne nation was arriued, and that they seemed rather Angels (in shape) then any earthly   20
creatures.

The Knight of the Castle hearing this, came downe and met them
in a large square Court paued with marble stone,/where hee kindly gaue [K2ᵛ]
them entertainement, promising them both lodging and other needfull
things they were destitute of.   25

The three Trauellers accepted of his courtesies, and being long before weather-beaten on the Seas, thought themselues from a deepe dungeon of calamities lifted to the toppe of all pleasures and prosperitie; thus
from this paued Court the Knight led them vp to his owne Chamber,
wherein was a fire made of Iuniper wood and Frankinsence, which   30
smelled very sweete: the walles were hung about with rich Tapestrie,
whereon was writ the story of Troyes destruction, the Creation of man-

kind, and the fearefull description of the latter day of Doome: likewise
hung vpon the said wales, Instruments of all sorts of musicke, with such
varietie of other pleasures, as they had neuer seene the like.

Now while these weary Trauellers tooke pleasure in beholding these
5 things, the good Knight caused his Dwarffe (which was all the seruants
that hee kept) to couer the Table, made of Cypresse wood, with a fine
Damaske table-cloth, and thereon set such dellicates as his castle afforded;
which was a piece of a wild Bore, rosted the same morning, with diuers
other seruices of Fowles, whereof the Countrey had plentie: Their bread
10 was made of the Almonds mixed with Goates milke (for no corne grew
in this soyle) their Drinke, of the wilde grape, likewise mingled with
Goates milke, which is in my minde, accounted restoratiue: to this Banquet were the Trauellers placed, where hauing good stomackes, they
quickly satisfied hunger, and after began to chat of their aduentures,
15 what danger they indured by sea, and how luckily they arriued in that
Countrey, giuing the courteous Knight great thanks for his kindnesse.

On the other side, when the Banquet was ended, euery one rising
from the table, he tooke an Orphirian that hung by, and caused his
Dwarffe, to daunce after the sound thereof: the strings whereof hee him-
20 selfe strayned with such curiositie, that it mooued much delight, especially the Lady Anglitora, whose eyes and eares were as attentiue to the
Melody, as Hellens were to the inchaunting Musicke of the Grecian
Paris. In this kind of pleasure consumed they most part of the day, till/
[K3] the bright Sunne began greatly to decline, then the Blacke Knight in a
25 couragious spirit, said.

Sir Knight (for so you seeme to bee by your entertainement of
Strangers) this Carpet kind of pleasure I like not, it disagrees with my
young desires: the hunting of vntamed Tygers, the Tilts and Turnaments of Knights, and the Battels of renowned Warriours, is the glory I
30 delight in: and now considering no other aduentrous exercise, may bee
found in this Countrey, but only the hunting of Wilde beastes, I will
into the Forrest and by manhood fetch some wilde Venison for my mothers supper.

The Knight of the Castle (seeing his resolution) furnished him with

72

a hunting Iauelin, and so directed him to the Forrest, where most plentie
of such pleasures were: God be his good speed, for wee will leaue the
Blacke Knight in his exercise, and speake of the wanton affections of
Anglitora, and the Knight of the Castle, that they cast vpon each other:
a short tale to make, whereas two hearts make one thought, the bargaine   5
is soone made: the Knight of the Castle hauing not had the presence nor
societie of a Woman in seuen yeeres before, grew as wantonly minded,
as the Roman Tarquinius, when hee rauished the chast Lady Lucretia.
On the other side, Anglitora hauing the venome of disloyaltie, grew so
pliable to his desires, that at his pleasure hee obteined that loue which in   10
former times the Red-rose Knight aduentured his life for; she that in
former times was accounted the worlds admiration for constancie, was
now the very wonder of shame, and the by-word of modest Matrons:
this was the first dayes entrance into their wanton pleasures, which in all
daliance they spent till the Sunne had lost the sight of the Earth: then   15
expecting the returne of the Blacke Knight from Hunting, they sate as
demurely, as they had been the chastest liuers of the world; not a glance
of wantonnesse passed betwixt them, but all modest and ciuill behauiours;
in this sort stayed they attending for the returne of the Blacke Knight,
but all in vaine: for hauing a wilde Panther in chase, hee followed so   20
farre in the vnknowne Forrest, that hee lost himselfe, all that night
trauelling to finde the way foorth, but could not; sleepe/was to him as [K3ᵛ]
meate to a sicke man; his steps were numberlesse, like the starres of
heauen, or the sands of the Sea: his deuises for recouerie little preuailed,
the further hee went, the further hee was from returning: thus day and   25
night (for many dayes and nights) spent hee in these comfortlesse
trauailes; no hope cheered his heart, no comfort bore him company, but
his patient minde: and now at last, when hee saw all meanes frustrate,
hee resolued to liue and die in that sollitary Forrest: his foode hee made
of the Fruits of trees, his drinke of the cleare running water, his Bed   30
was no better then a heape of Sun-burnd Mosse, his Canopies the azure
Elements full of twinckling lights, his Curtaines a row of thicke branched
Trees, the Torches to light him to his Bed, the Starres of Heauen, the
Melodie or Musicke to bring him asleepe, the croakes of Rauens, or the

73

fearefull cries of night Owles: the Clocke to tell the houres of the night,
were hissing Snakes, and Toades croaking in foggy grasse: his morning
Cocke the cheerefull Nightingale, or the cherping Larke: his companions
on the day, were howling Woolues, rauening Lyons, and the wrathfull
5 Boares: all (as the Fates had decreed) as gentle to him in fellowship,
as people of a ciuill gouernment: for to say troth, time and necessitie had
conuerted him to a man of wild conditions: for his hayre was growne
long and shaggy, like vnto a Satyre: his flesh tanned in the Sunne as an
Indian: the nailes of his fingers were as the tallents of Eagles, wherewith
10 hee could easily climbe the highest trees: garments hee had not any, for
they were worne out, and as willingly was hee content with nakednesse,
as in former times hee was with rich habiliments.

Thus liued hee for seauen yeeres in this desolate Forrest, by which
time hee was almost growne out of the fauour of a man: where for a
15 time wee will leaue him, and proceed to other accidents; also wee will
ouer pass the leawd liues of Anglitora and the Knight of the Castle, nor
speake as yet any more of their seauen yeeres adulterie; for numberlesse
were the sinnes committed by them in those seuen yeeres, in that accursed
Castle.

CHAPTER 5

How the Red-ROSE Knight *found his* Lady,
and how he was most strangely murthered,
and buried in a dunghill.

THE BLACKAMORE SLAUE (as you haue heard) attended vpon
25 them, like an obedient Seruant, and shewed all dutie and loue, till Anglitora gaue her body to the spoyle of Lust, and from a vertuous Lady conuerted her selfe to a hated Strumpet, which vile course of life when the
Indian perceiued, hee secretly departed the Castle, greatly lamenting the
wrongs of his Master, the Red-rose Knight, whose noble minde deserued
30 better at her hands. Day and night trauailed the poore slaue toward Eng-

74

land, thinking to finde his Master there, and to reueale that which hardly hee thought would be beleeued by him: wearie and opprest with hunger went hee this long Iourney: many Prouinces hee passed through, before hee could learne the way towards England; and then was hee so farre from it, as at the first, when hee departed from the Castle. 5

The labouring Husbandman grieued not more to see his Corne and Cattle taken by Theeues: nor the Marchant to heare of his Shippes suncke at Sea, then did this Indian at his vaine trauels, and wearisome Iourneys to small purpose: so at last setting forward againe, hee came to the sea side, thinking to heare of some Shippe to giue him passage ouer: but alasse, 10 one crosse falls after another, one mischiefe comes vpon the necke of another: and one mischance seldome happens alone; so as this true hearted Negar stood beholding how the billowes of the Sea beate against her banckes, and the Whale fishes lay wallowing in the Waues: behold such a tempest suddenly arose, that by the force thereof, the poore slaue was 15 cast into the Sea: but by reason of his Silken vaile tyde about his middle, and his great skill in swimming, (as most Negars bee perfect therein) kept himselfe from / drowning: and as good fortune would, the same tem- [K4ᵛ] pest droue the weather-beaten shippe to the same shore wherein the Red-rose Knight (his master) was, which Shippe had beene seuen yeares 20 vpon the Sea in great extreamitie, and before this tyde could neuer see land. By that time the tempest ended, the Shippe floted to land, wherein was left but onely the Red-rose Knight in his Palmers weede (for all the rest were starued vp for want of food) who being weake and feeble, climbed to the top of the Hatches, where when hee had perceiued the 25 Negar labouring for life vpon the waters, cast out a long coard, and so saued him: whome when the Red-rose Knight saw, and perfectly knew, hee fell all most into a traunce for ioy, supposing his Lady and Sonne not to bee farre distant: but recouering his former senses, hee spake as followeth. 30

Oh blessed Neptune, hast thou vouchsafed to deliuer mee from the depth of thy bowels, and cast mee on land, where once againe I may behold my Anglitora, and my deare Sonne, the Blacke Knight. These seuen yeares famine indured on the Sea, hath beene a sweete pleasure to mee, in that the end brings mee to my desires. Full threescore of my miserable Companions in this Shippe, hath death seazed vpon, and through Famine, haue eaten one another, making their hungry bowels graues for the others Carcases; and though now this belly of mine (like the Canibals) haue 5 beene glutted with humane flesh, and this mouth of mine tasted the blood of man: yet am I as pittiful as the tender hearted Mother, forgetting her Sonnes offences: and to my Anglitora will bee as kinde, as if neuer shee had trespassed: nor like the Grecian Helina, left her marryed Lord: So taking the Blackamoore by the hand, hee demaunded of her welfare, 10 and in what estate his Sonne remayned? The true hearted Negar could hardly speake for griefe, or vtter one word for teares: yet at the last with a wofull sigh, hee vttered foorth these heart-killing speeches.

O my noble Maister (quoth hee) by you from a Pagan I was made a Christian: by you, from a Heathen nation without ciuilitie, I was [L] brought to a Land of Princely go-/uernment; and by you till my departure, was I maintained in good manner: therefore if I should proue a periured slaue, and a false Varlet towards you, my body were worthy to bee made foode for hungry Fowles of the Ayre, and for the rauening Beasts of the Fields: therefore now considering that duty bindes mee to 20 it, I will reueale such wofull chaunces, and such disloyall trickes shewed by your Lady as will make your heart tremble, your Sinewes shake, and your haire to stand vpright. Anglitora your Lady and Wife, hath dishonoured your Bed and polluted that sacred Chamber of secrecie, which none ought to know, but onely you two: That mariage vow shee made 25 in Gods holy Temple, hath shee infringed, and vntyed the knot of Nuptiall promise: in a Countrey farre from hence hath shee wrought this hated crime: in a Countrey vnpeopled liues shee in a Castle, which is kept by a Knight of a wanton demeanour; there liue they two in adultery, there liue they secreatly sleeping in wantonnesse: and therefore these 30 seauen yeares hath shee made her selfe the childe of shame: All this with extreame griefe doe I vnfold, and with a heart almost kilde with sorrow, doe I breath out the dutie of a seruant: if I haue offended, let my death make amends: for what I speake is truely deliuered from a heart vnfaigned.

All this time of this his sorrowfull Discourse, stood the Red-rose Knight in a bitter agonie, like one newlie dropt from the cloudes, not knowing how to take these discourtesies: one while purposing to bee reuenged, and with his nailes to teare out the Strumpets eyes: another while, bewayling her weake nature, that so easily was woon to lewd- 5 nesse: but at last, taking to him (the vertue) patience, hee resolued to trauell to the Castle, and with his meek perswasions seeke to winne her from her wickednesse, and to forget, forgiue, and cast out of remem- brance all these her vnwoman-like demeanours, obseruing the Prouerbe, That faire meanes sooner winnes a woman, then foule. Thus in company 10 of his true seruant the Negar, hee tooke his iourney toward the Castle; where (after foure moneths trauell) they ariued; the Red-rose Knight, by the directions of the Negar, knocked, and in his Pilgrimes habite, de- sired meate and lodging for himselfe and his guide./

The first that opened the Gate, was his owne Lady, who immedi- [Lᵛ] ately, vpon the sight of them blushed, as though some sodaine feare had affrighted her; yet dessemblingly (colouring her knowledge of them) shee in a charitable manner gaue them entertainement and con- ducted them to a by roame at the backe side of the Castle: into which place shee sent them (by her Dwarffe) victuals from her owne Table, with a 20 commaund, that the next morning they should auoyde, and neuer more trouble that place.

This message sent by the Dwarffe, much disquieted the Red-rose Knight, and droue such amaze into his minde, that hee grew ignorant what to doe: And seeing his appointed time very short to remaine there, 25 hee now thought fit to strike whilst the Iron was hotte, and to discouer what hee was: so taking the Scarffe of Iewells and Rings tyed to his left side against his heart (which shee knew perfectly well to bee the giftes of her Loue) and by the Dwarffe sent them her: The which no sooner shee beheld, but shee openly sayd to thee Knight of the Castle, that 30 their secret affections were discouered, and her Husband in the habite of a Palmer made abode in her House conducted thither by the Moore, to bring their shame to light, and to carry her thence to England, there to be punished for her sinnes. Heereupon the Knight and shee purposed

77

the same night to rid themselues of that feare, and by some violent death sende the Palmer to his last abyding. Disquietnesse attended on all sides for that day, and euery houre seemed ten, till night approached; which at last came, though long lookt for. Then Anglitora in company of the
5 Knight of the Castle, like vnto Murtherers, rose from their Bedds, euen at that houre of night when mischiefes are acted, when no noyse was heard but the barking of Wolues, the howling of Dogges, and the croaking of Night-owles; all assistants to blacke actions: In this manner came they into the Lodging of the Palmer who for wearinesse of his Iourneyes,
10 most soundly slept, little dreaming that such crueltie, could be lodged in the boosome of his wedded Wife: one whose loue he had first gained with great daunger, and alwayes esteemed as deare as his owne heart
[L2] blood. All signes of duty/had shee obscured, not any remembrance had shee of Womanhood: Marriage Loue was forgotten, their passed ioyes
15 were as things neuer been: not any thought of remorse remayned within her; but shee more cruell then the new deliuered Bear, or the Tyger starued for meate, by the helpe of the Knight of the Castle, tooke the Scarffe of Iewells (sent her from him the same euening) and by violence thrust them downe the Palmers throat: by which meanes they bereaued
20 him of life and without any solemnity due to so braue a man, they buried him in a Dunghill without the Gate, not shedding so much as one teare for his death: so great was the envie of this his spitefull Lady. The poore Negar they set vp to the middle in the ground so surely fastned, that by any meanes he could not stirre from thence, where wee will leaue him wish-
25 ing for death. The Red-rose Knight, or rather the vnhappy Palmer, in his vnchristian like Graue, and the Knight of the Castle with the murtheresse Anglitora, to their surfetting Banquets of sinne, and returne to the Blacke Knight, which had lost himselfe in the Woods.

CHAPTER 6

How the Blacke Knight *being lost in a wilder-*
nesse became a wild man, how his Fathers
Ghost *appeared vnto him, and in what man-*
ner hee slew his owne Mother.   5

BY THIS TIME the Blacke Knight grewe so naturall a Wilde-man
as though hee had beene bredde in the Wildernesse: for day by day hee
sported with Lions, Leopards, Tygers, Elephants, Vnicornes, and such
like kinde of Beasts, playing as familiarly with them, as in King Arthurs
Court hee had done with gallant Gentlemen. But marke how it hapned   10
one day aboue an other: Hee chaunced to walke downe into a Vally,
where hee set himselfe downe by the Riuers side, and in humane complaints bewayled his owne estate, how beeing borne and bred of a/
Princely Race, discended royally should thus consume his dayes in sauage [L2ᵛ]
sort, amongst Wilde beasts, and by no meanes could recouer his libertie, 15
or free himselfe from that solitary Wildernesse. Being in this distresse
of mind, a suddaine feare assayld him, his heart shiuered, his haire stood
vpright, the Elements seemed to looke dimme, a terrible Tempest tore
vp huge trees, the Wilde Beastes roared and gathered on a heape together,
Birdes fell liuelesse from the ayre, the Ground as it were trembled, and   20
a sodaine alteration troubled each thing about him: in this amaze sate
hee a good time, maruelling what would ensue; at last there appeared
(as hee imagined) the Ghost of his Father newly murthered with a countenance pale and wan, with hollowe eyes (or none at all) gliding vp
and downe before him: casting such fearefull frownes, as might make   25
the stoutest heart in the world to tremble: and at last, setting himselfe
before the Blacke Knight, spake as followeth.

Feare not my Sonne, I am the Ghost of thy murthered Father, returned from Plutoes hollow Region: I came from that burning Kingdome where continually flames an euerlasting Furnace: from the   30
fearefull Pitte come I to thee for reuenge: Oh thou my Sonne, if euer
gentle Nature were plyant in thy boosome: if euer thou tookest pleasure

to heare thy Fathers honours spoken of; if euer thou desirest to haue thy
life meritorious in this world, take to thee thy neuer failing Courage,
and reuenge my death vpon thy adulterous Mother: thy Mother now
liuing in the filthinesse of shame, making the Castle where shee now
5 remaines in, a lustfull stewes; there was I murthered, and there buried
in a stincking Dunghill; no man gaue mee Funerall teares, nor any sor-
rowed for my death: I that haue dared Death in the face, and purchast
Honour in many Kingdomes, was slaine by my owne Wife, by my neerest
Friend, by my second selfe, by Anglitora, by her whom the whole world
10 admired for vertue: Rise (deare Sonne) rise, and hast thee to that Castle
polluted with the shame of thy wicked Mother: Rise I say, and let the
Pauements of that Castle, be sprinkeled with their detested blood, the
[L3] blood of that Monster that/hath not onely dispoyled my marriage bedde
of honoured dignities, but like a tyrant to her owne flesh hath murthered
15 mee. See how the angry Heauens (as it were) doe threaten my Reuenge:
hearke how Hell-Furies doe howle and roare for Reuenge: my Wiues
Adulterie at the hand of Heauen deserues Reuenge: My bleeding soule
(Oh my Sonne) wandreth in vnquiet paths, till thou workest Reuenge:
my death and murther cries (as did the blood of Abell) for Reuenge:
20 then feare not (Sonne) to act it; for duty, loue and nature bindes thee
to it. By Heauen, and by that great immortall Throane of happinesse:
By that low Kingdome of eternall paines; By the huge watrey Seas I
past to follow her: By Earth and by the Soules of all the mortall men that
euer dyed, I commaund, charge, and constraine thee to perseuere in this
25 Reuenge: Hence to that foule defamed Castle, defamed by Adulterie,
defamed by Murther; there to my Soule doe thy latest dutie: there,
wound thy cursed Mothers breast, there sacrifice her liues blood, there
appease thy Fathers Ghost insenst with furie; so shall my Soule in ioy,
enter the Fields of faire Elizeum: But if thou prouest coward-like, and
30 through feare deny to execute my glorious Reuenge, from this day
hence-forth shall my pale, wan, leane, and withred Ghost with gastly
lookes, and fearefull steps, pursue and follow thee. These were the words
of his Fathers Ghost: and hauing spoken these words, with a grieuous

groane, hee vanished. At this his sodaine departure, the Blacke Knight cryed with a loud and fearefull voyce, saying.

My noble Father, stay; Oh stay thy hasty steppes: once more let mee heare thee speake. Whether flyest thou? Oh let me heare thy voyce againe: It will not be, He is vanished; and my Mother liues as a shame 5 to all our generation. Oh thou staine of woman-hood: Oh thou bloody Lionnesse: Oh brutish act: Oh beastly desires: Where shall I now finde a place to shed teares in? for my heart is rent into tenne thousand pieces, and the terrour of this deed, is too intolerable. Rest thou in peace, sweete Father: thou in thy life wert both wise and valiant: thy vertue, wisedome, 10 and man-/hood made thy very enemies to loue thee: Oh then, what for- [L3ᵛ] tune hadst thou, to die by the friendly trust of thy owne Wife, my dis-loyall Mother, thy neerest friend prou'd thy greatest enemie; and by a Womans mallice, that heart was killed, that millions of Foes could neuer daunt. Oh sweete Red-rose Knight, most happy hadst thou been to haue 15 dyed in the Fields of bloody Warre, and seal'd thy liues quittance amongst renowned Souldiers: then had thy death beene more honorable, my wicked Mother had not murthered thee, nor I been inforst to take such bloody vengeance, as I intend (deare Father) for thy sake: for let mee neuer breath one day longer, nor view the next Mornings rising Sunne: 20 let mee neuer liue imprisoned in this Wildernesse, let nothing prosper that euer I take in hand, and here let the worlde end, if I cease to prosecute a mortall Reuenge, as the soule of my Father hath commaunded. Here-upon hee set forward toward the Castle, conducted by what chaunce the Heauens had allotted him: not one steppe hee knew aright, nor what 25 course to take to finde the direct way: but it hapned, that an ignis fatuus (as hee thought) or a goeing Fire, led him the right way out of the For-rest directly to the Castle where his dishonest Mother made her abode. But comming neere vnto the Gates, hee found all close, and neere vnto the Castle the Blackamoore set halfe way quicke into the earth, hauing 30 (for want of foode) eaten most part of the flesh from his armes; whom the Blacke Knight soone digged vp, and kept aliue, to be a furtherance to his intended reuenge.

The poore Indian, being thus happily preserued from death, reuealed all that had happned in the said Castle; how his Mother liued in adultery, how his Father was murthered, why himselfe was set quicke in the earth; and lastly, for the loue of his dead Master, hee protested to conduct him
5 through a secret Vault into the Castle, that in the dead of the night they might the easier accomplish their desired reuenge: Thus lingring secretly about the Castle till the middle of night: a time (as they imagined) to bee the fittest for their tragicall businesse: at last the midnight houre
[L4] came, and through a secret Cell they entred vnder the Castle into/the
10 Lodging where his Father was murthred. This is the place (quoth the Negar) where my sad eyes beheld thy Father both aliue and dead; so goeing from thence into the Chamber (which by chaunce, and as ill lucke had appointed) was through negligence left open, hee shewed him the Bedde where these Adulterers lay secretly sleeping in each others Armes.
15 Oh dolefull sight! This lust hath made mee fatherlesse, and ere long this Weapon shall make me motherlesse: so kneeling downe vpon his knees, in a whispering manner hee said vnto himselfe. Yee lowring Destinies, now weaue vp the Webbe of their two liues that haue lived too long. You infernall Furies, draw neere: Assist me thou reuengefull God Nemesis,
20 for on this Sword sits now such a glorious Reuenge, as being taken, the world will applaude mee for a louing Sonne. Hauing spoken these words, hee sheathed his Sword vp to the hiltes in the boosome of the Knight of the Castle, who lying in the armes of Anglitora, gaue so deadly a groane, that shee immediatly awaked: first looking to the Knight that was slaine
25 in her Armes, then perceiuing her Sonne standing with his weapon drawne, yet wreaking in the blood of the dead Knight, meanacing like-wise her death, with a wofull shrike she breathed out these words,

Oh what hast thou done my cruell Sonne? Thou hast slaine the miracle of humanitie; and one whom I haue chosen to be my hearts
30 Parramour, and thy second Father.

Oh Lady (quoth the Blacke Knight) for Mother is too proud a title for thee: what Furie driueth thee to lament the deserued death of that lewde blood shedder, and not rather choose with heart-renting sighes, to bewaile the death of my Father, thy renowned Husband, whose guiltlesse

82

body, euen dead, thou didst dispise, by burying him inhumanly vpon a dounghill; but Heauen hath graunted, and Earth hath agreed, detesting both thy misdeedes, and hath sent mee to sacrifice thy blood vnto the Soule of my murthered Father. Whilst hee was speaking these words, Anglitora arose from her bed, and in her smocke (which was of pure   5 Cambricke) shee kneeled to her sonne vpon her bare knees, saying.

Oh thou my deare Sonne, whom once I nourisht in/my painefull [L4ᵛ] wombe, and fedde thee with mine owne blood, whom oft I choycely dandled in my armes, when with lullababyes and sweet kisses I rocked thee asleepe: Oh farre bee it from thee (my louing Sonne) to harme that   10 breast, from whom thou first receiuest life: Of thee (my Sonne) thy Mother beggeth life. Oh spare the life, that once gaue thee life, with bleeding teares, I doe confesse my wanton offences, I doe confesse through mee thy Father dyed: Then, if confession of faults may merit mercie, pardon my life. Obscure not thy renowne with cruelty, making thy selfe   15 vnkind and monstrous in murthering of thy Mother. I charge thee, by thy dutie that thou owest mee, by all the bondes of loue betwixt a Mother and a Sonne, by all the kindnesse shewed to thee in thy infancy, let thy mother liue that begs life vpon her bare knees: Doe not thou glory in my miseries: let not my teares whet on thy cruellnesse: let not thy minde   20 bee bent to death and murther: bee no sauage Monster: bee not vnnaturall, rude and brutish: let my intreaties preuaile to saue my life: wound not the wombe that fostred thee, which now I tearmed wicked, by onely fostring thee; what childe can glut his eyes with gazing on his Parents wounds, and will not faint in beholding them.   25

Hereupon the Blacke Knight not able to indure to suffer his Mothers further intreaties, least pittie and remorse might mollifie his heart, and so graunt her life (which to Heauen to take away hee had deepely sworne) hee cut her off with these deadly words.

Lady, I am not made of Flint nor Adamant; in kinde regard of   30 calamitie, I am almost strucke with remorce: but dutie must quite vndoe all dutie: Kinde must worke against kinde, all the powers of my body bee at mortall strife, and seeke to confound each other, Loue turnes to Hatred: Nature turnes to wrath, and Dutie to Reuenge: for mee thinkes

my Fathers Blood with a groning voice, cryes to Heauen for Reuenge: therefore to appease my Fathers angry spirit, here shalt thou yeeld vp thy deerest blood. Here was hee ready to strike, and with his sword to finish vp the tragedie: but that his grieued soule in kinde nature plucked back
[M] his/hand: whereupon with a great sigh he sayd.

Oh Heauens; how am I grieued in minde. Father forgiue mee, I cannot kill my Mother. And now againe, mee thinks I see the pale shaddow of my fathers Ghost glyding before mine eyes; mee thinkes hee shewes me the manner of his murther; mee thinkes his angry lookes threaten
10 mee and tels how that my heart is possest with cowardice, and childish feare; Thou doest preuaile, O Father euen now receiue this sacrifice of blood and death; this pleasing sacrifice, which to appease thy troubled soule, I heare doe offer. And thus in speaking these words, with his Sword hee split the deare heart of his mother; from whence the blood as from
15 a gushing Spring issued. Which when hee beheld, such a sodaine conceit of griefe entred his minde, considering that hee had slaine his owne Mother, whom in duty hee ought to honour aboue all liuing women, that hee rather fell into a frenzie then a melancholy; and so with a pale countenance and gastly lookes, with eyes sparkling like to a burning
20 Furnace, began to talke idlely.

What haue I done? Whome hath my bloody hand murthered? Now woe vnto my soule for I am worse then the Viperous brood that eates out their Dammes wombe to get life vnto themselues: they doe but according to nature, I against all Nature; for I haue digged vp the boosome that first
25 gaue mee life. Oh wicked wretch; where shall I nowe hide my head? for I haue slaine my selfe, in killing her: I haue staynde this Chamber heere with humane blood. The Heauens abhorre me for this deed: The World condemnes mee for this murther, and Hell Furies will follow mee with shame and terrour: The Gods are grieued, Men (me thinks)
30 flie my company: dead Ghosts arise in my distresses: I see my Mother comes with a brest bleeding, threatning confusion to my fortunes. Oh thou vgly Spirit, cease to follow mee, torment me not aliue, for the wrath of Heauen is fallen vpon my head. Dispaire, where art thou? I must finde thee out, I will goe seeke thee through the world: and if in the

84

world I finde thee not, Ile saddle winged Pegasus, and scale the mantion place of Ioue. I will ransake all the corners of/the skie. I will throwe [Mᵛ] downe the Sunne, the Moone, and Starres: then leauing heauen, I will goe seeke for Despaire in the loathsome poole of Hell; there in Plutoes Court will I binde blacke Cerberus vp in Chaines, the triple-headed Hel-   5 hound, that Porter of Hell gates, because hee let Despaire passe from thence. In this frantike sort ranne he vp and downe the Chamber, and at last with the nayles of his fingers hee fell to graue vpon the Stone walles the picture of his Mother, imitating Pigmalion, hoping to haue life breathed into the same. Meane while the poore Indian with fleshlesse   10 armes heaued vp towards Heauen, and on his bare knees, made his suppli-cation to the Gods, for the Blacke Knights recouery of his wittes.

Oh you angry Heauens (quoth hee) reuoke your heauy doomes, for-get this crime, forgiue this vnnaturall murther: pittie the state of this distressed Knight, and send some meanes to recouer his senses. Thou   15 bright Lampe of Heauen, thou eternall light, although in iustice we haue deserued thy wrath, yet let my prayers, my neuer ceasing Prayers, my heartes renting Sighs, my deepe inforced Teares, worke some remorce from thy incensed ire, that either this Knight may recouer his lost senses, or set him free from death. Thus in a zealous manner prayed the poore   20 Negar, desiring God to lay the Knights fault vpon his head, and reclaime his vnbridled rage; which Prayer was soone regarded by Heauen, for the Blacke Knight had immediatly his madnesse turned into a sad melan-cholly; and in a more gentle manner made his sad lamentations, as you shall heare in the next Chapter.   25

But now the Negar, that all the time of Anglitoras murther stood in a traunce, beganne now a little (considering the fright hee tooke at the Blacke Knights madnesse) to summon againe together his naturall senses; and perceiuing the vnchast Lady dead, cold, pale, wanne, lying weltering in her goare, and the blood of her false heart (shed by her owne   30 child) all besprinckled about the Chamber, sayd as followeth.

Now (quoth the Negar, betwixt life and death) haue you showne your selfe a dutifull Sonne, and nobly reuenged the death of your Father. These were the last words of the poore/Indian; which as then sanke [M2]

downe, and neuer after breathed. Thereupon came foorth the Dwarffe of the Castle, with great store of treasure, proffering the same to the Blacke Knight; who nothing thirsting after couetousnesse, refused it, and withall tooke the Dwarffe in satisfaction for the Negars death, and
5 crammed the treasure downe his throate; and after buryed the two Seruants together in one Graue. This being done he digged vp his Fathers body from the Dunghill, and brought it to the Chamber where his mother lay and after in an Abby yard belonging to the Castle, he buryed them both likwise, in one Graue. This being done, hee kneeled thereupon,
10 and made his complaint in this manner.

CHAPTER 7

Of the Black Knights *melancholy lamentations ouer the graue of his* Parents; *and of other things that hapned.*

15 OH THRICE HAPPY foreuer-more bee this ground that containes the bodyes of my vnfortunate Parents; for this Earth hath receiued the sweete Darling of Nature, and the onely delight of the whole World; the Sunshine of Christendome, and the glory of Mankinde: Oh thrice happy be the grasse, that from hencefoorth shall grow vpon this Graue: let neuer
20 Sithe touch it, nor crafty lurking Serpent with venemous breath, or deadly poyson, hurt it: Let no Lyons pawes, nor Beares feet, tread vpon it: Let no Beastes Horne in any manner abuse it: Let no Birds with pecking, nor creeping filthy Vermine, no winters nipping Frost, no nightly falling Dewes, no rage of the parching Sunnes heate, nor Starres, haue power
25 from Heauen: nor fearefull Tempest nor horrible Lightning, in any manner annoy it: Let no Plough-man driue hither his weary Oxen, nor Shepheards bring hither their Sheepe, least by the Bulls rage it bee harmed, or by the harmelesse Sheepe it be eaten: but let it for euer grow, that the displaying thereof may reach to Heauen: and may from hence-
[M2ᵛ] foorth/this Graue be euer accounted sacred: and may the Grasse bee

86

euer sprinkled with sweet Waters. Some good man vpon this Graue set
a burning Taper, that then for euery anguish of my heart, I may beate
my Breasts, till my Fistes haue strucken the winde from my body; and
that my Soule may beare them company in Elizium. Come you wanton
fleshly Satyres: Come you friendly Fawnes: Come you Fayries and Dry-   5
ades, and sing sweet Epitaphes; lift vp your voyces to Heauen, and let
your prayses bee in the honour of my Parents: my selfe like a wan, pale,
and dead man, will beare you company: I will wearie the World with
my complaints: I will make huge Streames with my Teares: such
Streames, as no Banke shall barre: such Streames, as no Drought shall   10
drye. But alasse what doe I meane to repeate these seuerall lamentations:
since my deare Parents bee dead: since from the world they are parted:
since they are buried without solemnitie: since my delights are all inclosed in the Grounde: yet will I still here make my complaints, though
no good ease comes thereby, adding teares to teares, and sorrowes to   15
sorrowes. Oh frowning Fortune. Oh vnlucky Starres. Oh cursed day that
euer I did this deed, for now no sence, nor knowledge, takes their vnsen-
sible bodyes of my griefes: in this Graue there is no feeling: in Death there
is no pittie taken. Oh thou Siluannus thou commander of these Mountaines, helpe mee poore helplesse soule to shed teares: for my religion,   20
for my deuotion and Countries sake helpe mee: either let me haue some
comfort in my sorrowes or let me in Death beare my Parents company.
Thou seest what Torments I suffer; how my heart trembles, how my
eyes flow with teares, how my head is with teares possest, how my Soule
is full of horrible anguish: all this thou seest, and yet it little grieues thee   25
to see it. Oh thou churlish ground, from hencefoorth cease any more to
beare Fruit: cease to be deck't with Flowers, cease to be mantled in
Greene, for the purest Flowers are withered. Thy Garlands are decayed:
my deare Parents are too vntimely bereft of life: their sweete bodyes thou
harborest, and in thy wombe deliueredst them as a food vnto/Wormes. [M3]
Therefore thou cruell Earth, howle and mourne, for thou art vnworthy
of such blessed bodies. And now, oh you pittifull Heauens, heare my complaints, conuey them to the Soules of my deceased Parents: for my lamentations by the gentle Windes, are blowen from the East vnto the West:

87

the dry Land, and the Watry Seas, are witnesses to them: Therefore no day shall rise, but it shall heare my complaints: no night shall come, but it shall giue eare vnto my moanes: neither day nor night, shall be free from my heart-breaking cryes. If that I groane, mee thinkes the Trees
5 are bended, as though they pittied my teares. The very Ground (for griefe) I see alters her complexion. All that I heare, all that I see, all that I feele, giues fresh increase to my sorrow. I will neuer henceforth come in peopled Towne, nor inhabited Cittie, but wander all alone vp and downe by low Vallyes, and steepy Rockes: or I will dwell in darke
10 Dennes frequented onely by Wilde Beastes, where no path of man was euer seene, or to the Woods I will goe, so darke, and beset so thicke with shaddowy branches, that no Sunne may shine there by day, nor no Starre by night may be seene, whereas is heard no voyce, but the outcryes of horrible Goblings, the balefull shrikes of Night-owles, the vnlukie sounds
15 of Rauens and Crowes; there shall mine eyes bee made watry Foun-taines; there will I make such plaints, as Beasts shall mourne to heare them: such plaints will I make, as shall rend and riue strong trees, make wilde Panthers tame, and mollifie hard flinty stones: And if by chance that sleepe oppresse mee, on the bare and cold Ground shall these wofull
20 limbs rest: the greene turffe shall serue as a Pillow for my head: boughs and branches of trees shall couer me: and then I hope, some venemous Serpent will speedily giue mee my deaths wound, that this my poore soule may be released from flesh and blood: by which meanes I may passe to those Fields, those faire Elizium Fields, whereas my murthered
25 Parents daily resort. In this manner complained the Blacke Knight vpon his Parents graue, three dayes and nights together, still kneeling vpon the cold ground and could not by any imagination bee comforted: euery
[M3ᵛ] thing/his eyes beheld, renewed fresh sorrow, and drew on new lamenta-tions: but at last, the Powers of Heauen intending to graunt him some
30 ease, cast his distressed Senses into a quiet slumber: where lying vpon his fathers graue, wee will let him for a time rest.

CHAPTER 8

How the Fayerie Knight *came to be called the*
Worlds Triumph, *Of his ariuall in* England,
of the two Knights *deaths, and of the* Pro-
uerbe *vsed of three* Cities *in* England.   5

YOU HAVE READ in the first part of this Historie, how the Fayerie
Knight the Sonne of Caelia, begot by the Red-rose Knight, was committed (by his Mother at her death) to the keeping of the Ladies of the
Land: for then were there but few Men liuing, being a Countrey onely
of Women: and now being of lusty age, and a Knight of renowned val-   10
oure, he betooke himselfe to trauell: the onely cause, to finde his Father,
or some of his kindred whom he had neuer seene.

Many were the Countries he passed: but more the dangers hee indured: all which for this time, wee omit: onely a little speake of three
guifts giuen him by an Hermite, that had three exceeding Vertues: For   15
comming to an Iland to seeke aduentures, it was his chance to saue a
young beautifull Mayden from rauishing by a satyricall Wild-man: for
he hauing tyed the golden locks of her Hayre to two knotty brambles,
and being ready to take his venerall pleasure vpon her, the Fayerie
Knight comming by, and seeing that dishonour and violence offered to so   20
young a Virgin, with his Sword at one blow, paired away the Wild-mans
head, and so went with the Mayden home to her Fathers house, which
was an Hermitage some mile distant off: where being no sooner come,
but the good old man, hauing a Head more white then Siluer, but a heart
more heauier then Lead, by reason of the/want of his daughter, so cruel-   [M4]
ly taken from him, began at her sight to be so cheered, that he had not
the power (for ioy) to speake a good space, but at last, taking the Fayerie
Knight by the hand, he led him to an inward roome, where hee ban-
queted him with such cheere as his Hermitage afforded; and after in
lieu of his daughters reschew, hee gaue him three such Gifts, and of three   30
such Vertues, as the like seldome had Knight. The first was a Ring,
which whosoeuer did weare, should neuer dye by treason. The second a

Sword; that on what Gate soeuer it strucke, it would presently fly open. The third and last, a viall of such Drinke that whosoeuer tasted, should sodainely forget all passed sorrowes.

Hauing receiued these three Gifts of the good old Hermite, he de-
5 parted, and trauelled without any aduenture till he came and found the blacke Knight asleepe vpon his fathers Graue: which when the Fayerie Knight had awaked, in countenance they were so alike, as Nature had made them both one, (for indeed they were Brothers by the Fathers side, the one true borne, the other a Bastard) yet at the first sight, such a secret
10 affection grew betwixt them, that they plighted their faythes to each other, vowing neuer to part friendships. But when the Blacke Knight had reuealed his birth and parentage, his Fathers name, and place of birth, the Fayerie Knight resolued himselfe, that he had found a Brother, as well in nature as condition: But when hee heard the story of his Fa-
15 thers life, and the manner of his death, with the murther of Anglitora his vnchast wife, hee could not choose but shed teares, whereof plenty descended from his faire eyes: whereupon hee tooke occasion to speake as followeth.

Heauen rest thy sweet soule (my vnknowne Father,) and may the
20 fruite of thee proue as famous in the World as thou hast been; but more fortunate in their Mariage choyse: As for my Stepmother, though her vnchast life hath made her infamous to all Womankinde, yet this in charitie I desire, that when shee comes to Plutoes Realme, that Proserpine may send her to the blessed fields of Elizium; in remembrance of whom,
25 in this world, (if euer we ariue in that noble Countrey of England,
[M4ᵛ] where my Knightly Father was/borne,) wee will there erect her a state-ly Tombe: yet no Epitaph shall show her disloyall life, nor the cause of her death: onely in Letters of beaten Gold, shall remaine ingrauen vpon her Tombe, the name of, Anglitora Daughter to Prester Iohn, and Wife
30 to the worthy Red-rose Knight. Hereupon hee gaue his new-found Brother (the Blacke Knight) his Viall of Drinke which the Hermit had giuen him: who no sooner had tasted, but all former greefes were for-gotten: hee remembred not the death of his Father, nor the murther of his Mother, nor what sorrow hee had sustayned in the Wildernesse: but

90

like a ioconde Knight, gyrt his Sword round about him, and stood on
Thornes till hee was set forward to seeke Martiall aduentures. Hereupon
these two Knights departed toward England, and performed many noble
deeds of Chiualrie by the way: But amongst all others, being in the Turkish Court (this is worthy to bee noted) for with one Boxe of the eare,   5
the Blacke Knight killed the Turkes Sonne starke dead: for which cause,
by treason were their liues conspired, and the following night had their
Lodging entred by twelue of the Turkes Guard, with an intent to murther them: but by reason of the inchaunted Ring, in the which they put
both their little fingers, the Guard of a sodaine fell all fast in a traunce: 10
hereupon the two Knights departed the Turkish Court. But no sooner
were they out of the Citie, but a troupe of armed Knights pursued them,
and followed them so neerely, that they were forced to enter a Castle
that stood by the Sea side, wherein no creature had abyding: comming to
the Gate, the Fayerie Knight with his Sword strucke thereat, and it   15
presently opened: wherein being no sooner entred, but the armed Knights
of the Turkish nation closed them fast in, and caused the Gates to bee
walled vp with Free Stone, and so departed. Now were these two Knights
in more danger of death, then euer they had beene in all their liues: and
sure they had starued, had not good pollicie preserued their liues: for the   20
Castle walles were so high, that none durst venture downe without great
danger. As in greatest extreamity, mans wit is the quickest for inuention:
so the two Knights cut off all the Hayre from/their heads (which were   [N]
very long) and therewithall made a long twisted Line or Cord, with
the which they slid from the top of the Wall to the Ground. But this mis-   25
chaunce hapned; as the Fayerie Knight glyded downe, the Coard broke,
and his body tooke such a violent blow against the stonie Ground, that it
strucke the breath quite out of his body; no life by the Blacke Knight
could bee perceiued, but that his soule was for euer diuided from his body.
This of all misfortunes, was held the extreamest; therefore in great griefe   30
hee breathed foorth this lamentation.

Oh you partiall Fates (quoth hee) Oh you vniust Destinies: Why
haue you reft two liues by wounding one? Now let the Sunne forbeare
his wonted light. Let Heate and Coulde, let Drought and Moysture, let

Earth and Ayre, let Fire and Water, be all mingled and confounded together: let that old confused Chaos returne againe, and heere let the World end. And now you Heauens this is my request, that my Soule may presently forsake this flesh: I haue no soule of mine owne, for it is the
5 soule of the Fayerie Knight, for but one Soule is common to vs both: then how can I liue, hauing my Soule departed, which spightfull death hath now separated? Oh thou my Knightly brother, though the Fates deny to giue thee life, yet in spight of them Ile follow thee. You Heauens receiue this halfe soule of my true Friend and let not life and death part
10 vs; with Eagles wings will I flye after him, and in Ioues celestiall Throane ioyne with him in friendship. We two in life were but one; one will, one heart, one minde, one Soule made vs one: one life kept vs both aliue, one being dead, drawes the other vnto death: therefore, as wee liued in loue, so will we dye in loue; and with one Graue wee may interre
15 both our bodyes: How glorious and happy were my death, to dye with my beloued friend: Now doe I loath this life, in liuing alone without my deare Brother: whereupon drawing his Sword from his side, hee sayd.

Oh thou wofull Weapon, euen thou shalt be the meane, to ridde my soule from this prison of body. Oh faith vnfaigned; Oh hand of sacred
20 friendship; I am resolued both with the force of Heart, Hand, and
[N^v] Armes, to giue my Heart deaths/deadly wound; for now my noble Fayerie Knight, this blood I offer vp vnto thy Soule. But being ready with his Sword to pierce his owne heart, hee saw a liuely blood spread in his friends face, and those eyes that were so dolefully closed vp, began
25 now to looke abroad; and the countenance that was so pale and wan, receiued a fresh complexion: whereupon the Blacke Knight stayed from his desperate resolution, and from a bloody tragedian, became the recouerer of his brothers life; who after a while, began to be perfect sencible: so binding his bruzed bones together, they went a Shipboard on a Shippe
30 that lay at anchor at the next Port, making for England, so the next morning (the wind serued well) the Pilots hoysted sayle, merily floting on the waters.

Ten weekes had not passed toward the finishing of a yeere, before they ariued on the Chaulkie cliftes of England; vpon which they had no sooner set footing, but with their warme lippes they gently kissed the cold earth, This is the Land of promised glory (said the Fayerie Knight) to finde this Land I haue indured many miseries: to find this Land I haue passed many Countries, and in this Land, must I seale vp the last quittance of my life, here shal my bones rest, for I am lawfully descended from the   5 loynes of an English Knight: peace bee in my ende, for all my dayes haue beene spent in much trouble.

In such like discourses left they the shore side, and travayling further into the Land, they met with one of King Arthurs Knights, named Sir Launcelat Dulake, so old and lame that through his bruises in chiualry,   10 hee seemed rather an impotent creature, then a Knight at Armes; yet at the sight of these two aduenturous Knights, his blood seemed to grow young: and hee that before, could not march a mile on foote for a King-dome, now went as liuely as any of the two other Knights did. First came they to London, where for their fathers sake, they were (by the Gouer-   15 nours) most gallantly entertained: the streets were hung round with Arras hangings, and Tapestrie workes: Pagiants were builded vp in euery street, the Conduits ran with Wine, and a solemne Holy-day was then proclaimed to be kept yearely vpon that day. To speake of Banquets prepared for them, the Tilts and Turnaments,/and such honourable [N2] graces, I thinke needlesse. In London in great content stayed they some twenty dayes: in which time came noble messengers from the Court to conduct them to the King that then raigned: for since the Blacke Knight and his mother departed the Land, hapned three changes, euery one maintaining the ancient honour of King Arthurs Knights of the Round   25 Table, whereof these two in presence of all the Nobilitie, were in Knightly sort created.

After this, the King ordained a solemne Iusting to be kept in his Court, and held in great honour for fortie dayes: to which Knightly sports, resorted the chiefest flowers of Chiualrie from all Countries, as   30 Kings, Princes, Dukes, Marquesses, Earles, Lords, and Knights; and for chiefe Challenger and Champion for the Countrey, was the Fayerie Knight: who for his matchlesse man-hood therein showne, had this title giuen him by a generall consent, to bee called, The Worlds Wonder.

93

After this, being desirous to see the Citie of Lincolne, where the Red-rose Knight was borne, hee in company of his Brother and true friend, the Blacke Knight, and old sir Lancelat Dulake, rod thither, at whose comming into the Citie, the great Bell (called Tom a Lincolne)
5 was rung an houre, which as then was seldome showne to any, excepting Kings, and renowned warriours, returning victoriously from bloody Battles. Here builded they a most sumptuous Minster, which to this day remaines in great magnificence and glory. Likewise here builded they a most stately Tombe in remembrance of their Parents: the like (as then)
10 no place of England afforded.

Thus hauing left the noble feats of Chiualry, they liued a life zealous, and most pleasing to God: erecting many Alms-houses for poore people, giuing thereto great Wealth and Treasure: And when nature ended their dayes, they were buried in the same Minster, both in one Tombe:
15 which likewise was so richly set vp with Pillars of Gold, that aboue all other Cities, it grew the most famous: whereupon since that time, hath this old Prouerbe of three Cities grown common, which is vsed in these words: Lincolne was, London is, and Yorke shall be.

FINIS

20   R. I.

94

Explanatory Notes*

PAGE	LINE	TEXT	EXPLANATION
3	3	WORTEDG	This man has left no record in any of the standard biographical references for the period.
	4	Okenberrie	almost certainly Alconbury, Huntingdonshire.
7	19	to humble when	Intr. used for refl.; for other occurrences see *OED*, V, 446.
8	3	pheere	(=fere) companion, friend.
8	30	remaine	for other occurrences see *OED*, VIII, 416.
9	8	quittance	recompense, payment.
9	30	glister	to glitter, shine.
9	34	Swaines	country or farm laborers, freq. shepherds.
10	16	incontinently	immediately, as soon as.
10	34	fatall Sisters	the three Fates, usually portrayed as sisters.
12	10	colours	usually as in its modern sense, i.e. pigments, but occasionally in the heraldic sense of badges, emblems, devices.
12	12	Barnsedale Heath	a famous haunt of outlaws. See J. Ritson, *Robin Hood* (London, 2nd ed., 1832), p. vii; also mentioned in a letter of Sir John Paston, 16

*In those of the following Notes which are merely glosses I have generally not glossed words which differ only in spelling from their modern equivalents, such as "scouling" (= scowling); "Semiter" (=scimitar); "tand" (=tanned); "Walles" (=Wales); and so forth. Except where some other source is noted, I have relied on the *Oxford English Dictionary* (Oxford, 1928, suppl. 1933), but I have only given definitions as they are habitually used in *Tom a Lincolne*.

April 1473 in reference to one of his servants, **W.** Woode:

> I have kept him this three years to play Saint George, and Robin Hood, and the Sheriff of Nottingham, and now when I would have good horse, he is gone into Bernysdale, and I without a keeper.

(From J. A. Fenn, ed., *The Paston Letters* [London, 1841], II, 78–9).

14	11	withall with.
14	12–13	Tom a Lincolne Tom's name came almost certainly from the common name for the Great Bell of Lincoln Cathedral.
14	28	Portingale 1. n., Portugal. 2. adj., Portuguese (Johnson lacked an adjectival form for Portugal, so he made the noun serve for both).
15	6	motion in Johnson's frequent use, an inward knowledge, prompting, inclination.
15	8	Lancelot du Lake, Sir Tristram, and Sir Triamore The same three knights figure in Middleton's *Chinon of England* (1597), where Johnson may have found them.
16	17	Armie mustered for Portingale It is possible that an actual contemporary British expedition (possibly one of Sir Francis Drake's occasional raids on the Portuguese coast) is being alluded to.
16	27	Charge and Quarter subdivisions, precincts, in this case of a military camp, such as company or battallion; here in the sense of "proper place," or "assigned area." See Shakespeare, *1 Henry VI* II.i.68; *Timon of Athens* V. iv. 60.
17	18	Champion flat and level. See *OED*, II, 260.
17	19	Lishborne Lisbon, capital of Portugal.
17	26	declining inclining, falling. See *OED*, III, 102.
18	21	Whiflers staff-bearers, from Minsheu's *Dictionary* (1617), quoted by Thoms in his reprint of *Tom a Lincolne* of 1828.

21	18	pretended intended, proposed.
22	14	inhabited onely by women For a discussion of Amazons in the literature of the period, see Celeste Turner Wright, "The Amazons in Elizabethan Literature," *SP*, XXXVII (1940), 433–456.
26	13	and acceptable grammar in 16th–17th C.
27	12	Adamants . . . steeled Heart Adamant is lodestone, i.e. a magnet, and her heart is drawn to it (him) because as a warrior, she is steeled. Apparently one of Johnson's favorite images, since he uses it also in Arthur's meeting with Angellica, where, of course, Arthur has the steeled heart.
30	5	[Sir Lancelot's tale] Despite the name Valentine being common to both, Lancelot's tale is not related to *Valentine and Orson*, a French romance translated c. 1550 by Henry Watson, which may, however, be the source of the Blacke Knight's transformation to a wild man in II,6. The actual source of Lancelot's tale is unknown, and it may be just conventional filler, but there are a significant number of parallels between this tale in Part I and the murder of Angellica by Arthur's widow in Part II.
32	33	dryerie dreary.
34	3ff	Notice similarities of this passage to *Cymbeline* I.v.4–44, in which the Queen asks the physician Cornelius for poison with which to murder her enemies, and instead is given a sleeping-potion which will not harm them. Since *Tom a Lincolne* was published in both parts by 1607, and the usual date given by scholars for *Cymbeline* is 1608–09, it would appear that Shakespeare may have been following either Johnson, or some source common to them both.
37	32	her may be an error for "his," but since both make sense, no emendation has been made.
38	26	Satire (see also 74:8 Satyre) a satyr, a wood-sprite rude, lascivious and aggressive in behavior. For a discussion of Renaissance views of the relationship

of satyr and satire, see Alvin Kernan, *The Cankered Muse* (New Haven, 1959), pp. 54–57 and 91–92.

38	34	**But now gentle Reader** Either Johnson has forgotten that this is Lancelot's narrative, and that he is telling it aloud, thus making references to a "reader" inappropriate, or Johnson has merely inserted the narrative at this point without having revised out such references.
41	12	**Prester Iohns Land** The legend of Prester John, an Eastern Christian potentate, was familiar at least since the publication of *Mandeville's Travels* (c. 1370), and is discussed at length in Vol. 5 of the Yale Edition of *The Works of St. Thomas More*, ed. John M. Headley (New Haven, 1969), pp. 929–31.
42	16	**Cressetts** metal vessels for holding grease or oil for light.
46	10–11	**a branch from the golden Tree** The well-known golden branch or bough originates in the *Aeneid*; for other Vergilian echoes see Caelia's death, possibly an echo of Dido's.
47	16–17	**washed the body** The washing of the hero is a well-known motif in folk-literature as well as in romance. It occurs most notably in the *Morte Darthur* [Book viii, chap. 9], in which Sir Tristram is put into the care of La Belle Isoud, whose attentions are more surgical than Anglitora's, though the effect in each story is similar.
49	12	**fardle** 1. n., originally one-quarter of anything, hence a small amount, bundle, etc. 2. v. t., to bundle, to make a bundle.
50	14	**kenning** sight.
52	26	**wishly** silently, steadfastly, occas. longingly.
60	7ff	The complete disregard which Johnson shows in this scene for Malory's version of Arthur's death (an event so important and dramatic that it gives his book its name) is almost evidence of Johnson's being ignorant of Malory's work altogether. It is difficult

to reconcile this sort of non-Arthurian death-scene with the apparent source-relationship mentioned in n.47:16–17 above. Perhaps Johnson obtained that material through some intermediate source which did not include Arthur's death. The alternative to this possibility is that Johnson was so concerned with telling his story of Arthur's adultery and confession that he prefers to show him as a concupiscent and self-satisfied burgher, rather than to inject a truly noble strain into his romance with an attempted recreation of Malory's scene.

62	30	Caparisons clothing, or more nearly, uniforms.
63	4	Morischo Moorish.
64	6	Princesse perhaps in the sense of Prince's.
64	13	Cockatrice (=Basilisk), a fabulous reptile which blasts objects by its glance.
64	18	sounde swoon.
64	21	sweat Though the variant *swate* in *1631* and *1635* may possibly be Johnson's attempt at an umlauted rather than dentalized past-tense form of *sweat* (the reading of *1655* here adopted), a printer's error in *1631* or its ancestor seems more likely.
65	12–13	Hero to her Leander . . . Pyramus to his Thisbie These are commonplace references to famous lovers, popularized by Ovid and Shakespeare among others, but widely known in popular tradition.
66	18	Arras worke tapestry.
66	31	writhen past. part. of writhe, therefore twisted, wrinkled.
67	28	Notice the similarities of the Queen's jealous murder of Angellica to Medea's jealous murder of Glauce, Jason's intended second wife, both of which were accomplished by means of poisoned garments. But as Euripides' play *Medea* was not available to Johnson, he must have found this material in some other representative of the legend, possibly Seneca's version, trans. Studley, 1566.

68	34	Anatomie a dissected cadaver.
70	15	riding knot a knot forming a noose which slides along the rope, tightening the noose when the rope is pulled.
70	24	Indian slaue Johnson seems confused about the slave's racial and national origin. On p. 63 he calls him a "Moore"; on 70–71 he is both an "Indian" and a "Blacke-amoor," and on 75 is an "Indian" and a "Negar." Johnson apparently thought that all dark-skinned people were identical, and therefore used for variety names that he considered synonyms. But compare his treatment of the more familiar Turks, p. 91 above.
72	18	Orphirian A stringed instrument made of metal having from 6 to 9 pairs of strings, which was much played in the 16th and 17th C.
73	8	Tarquinius ... Lucretia A commonplace reference to the figures popularized by Ovid and Shakespeare among others (see 65:12–13).
74	14	For literary background of the savage man theme, see Donald Cheney, *Spenser's Image of Nature* (New Haven, 1966).
77	5	woon 16th and 17th C. variant form of "won." For other occurrences see *OED.*
78	21	without outside.
81	26	ignis fatuus Literally, "silly fire," a phosphorescent light seen hovering or flitting over marshy ground, and supposed to be the result of the spontaneous combustion of inflammable gases [H_2S, etc.]. Formerly thought to be a mischievous sprite, occasionally leading travelers out of the right path, hence occasional figurative use. For many other occurrences see *OED.*
84	15–16	conceit conception, sense.
84	33–85:7	The Blacke Knight's rhetorical pursuit of despaire is very reminiscent of Hotspur's similar pursuit of honor in *1 Henry IV* I.iii.201–8. (1597–8).

87	19	Siluannus Roman god of uncultivated lands.
89	19	venerall For other examples of this obs. spelling, see *OED*.
90	10–11	They plighted their faythes to each other, vowing neuer to part friendships. For background on Renaissance ideas of friendship see L. J. Mills, *One Soul in Bodies Twain* (Bloomington, 1937).
91	6	Turkes Sonne The fascination that the East exerted over Elizabethan minds is treated in S. C. Chew's *The Crescent and the Rose* (New York, 1937). Since there was more commerce with the Ottoman empire than with most of the other Eastern nations, Johnson and other Londoners would be less likely to confuse Turks with Indians, than Indians with Moors, etc. See n. 70:24 above.
91	18	Free Stone Any fine-grained sandstone or limestone that can be cut or sawn easily.
93	17	Pagiants Any kind of show, device, or temporary structure, exhibited as a feature of a public triumph or celebration.
94	18	Lincolne was, London is, and Yorke shall be A proverb which Dekker referred to as "that worme-eaten prouerbe" in his *Wonderfull Yeare* (1603). If it was "worme-eaten" in 1603, it must have been at least well-worn in 1599, and entirely consumed by 1607, when Part II of *Tom a Lincolne* appeared.

Textual Notes

18 such kindnes,] such kindnesses *1635*, with kindnesses, *1655*

25 now] *Ed.*, how *1631 1635 1655*

30 remaine] remain *1655*

p. 9   1 furnishing] furnish *1655*

8 bore] poor *1655*

14 Fields] field *1635 1655*

17 reports] report *1655*

24 closely] disclosely *1655*

30 *No new paragraph 1655*

32 time,] time *1635 1655*

33 woonted] *1635 1655*, wanted *1631*

34 foorth] out *1655*

p. 10   4 greene] *om. 1655*

tooke] *1635*, took *1655*, take *1631*

5 parcell] part *1655*

7 necke] neck *1655*

8 time,] time *1635 1655*

19 who] *1635 1655*, whom *1631*

20 speake wee] we speak *1655*

p. 11   2 thirsted] *1635 1655*, thirsted for *1631*

16 sort; for] *1635 1655*, sort; (for *1631*

21 hee was of a valiant and inuincible courage] he was valiant, and of an invincible courage *1655*

22 his] the *1655*

25 superiour] *1655*, superious *1631 1635*

27 amongst] among *1635 1655*

p. 12   1 first,] first *1655*

them] them; *1655*

3 them:] them *1655*

6 the] there *1655*

9 seuerally] *om. 1655*

10 that] *om. 1655*

13 liued] liued a *1655*
14 were] was *1635 1655*
    greatly] *om. 1655*
17 him,] him *1655*
19 meane] means *1655*
21 taske] *1635 1655*, tasking *1631*
28 kind:] kind! *1655*
30 age:] age? *1635 1655*
32 estate?] *1635 1655*, estate: *1631*

p. 13   14 Sonne,] Son, *1635*, Son *1655*
            15 hands,] hands *1655*

p. 14   6 Knight.] *1635 1655*, Knight, *1631*
           11 pound] pounds *1655*
           28 first] *om. 1655*

p. 15   5 liuely] *om. 1655*
            6 motion] *1631 1635 1655 (see note)*
           15 Barnsedale] *Ed.*, Barnsedale *1635 1655*, Bransedale *1631*
           21 a hundred] an hundred *1655*
           22 best] *om. 1655*
           23 to] of *1655*
           30 commers.] commers, *1655*

p. 16   3 marke,] mark *1655*
            8 grew] grew, *1655*
            sware] swore *1655*
           11 vnborne,] unborne *1655*
           12 iust] *om. 1655*
           21 one,] one *1655*
           Captaines] Captainer *1655*
           23 knowne] *om. 1655*
           27 And] or *1635 1655*
           30 priuy] private *1635 1655*
           33 prowesse] *1635 1655*, pro esse *1631*

3 so] so, *1635*

7 danger,] danger *1635 1655*

8 moneths] Moneths *1655*

10 euer-changing] euer changed *1635 1655*˙

18 at] of *1655*

23 the Red-rose] the courageous and valiant Red-rose *1655*

24 vnderstoode] understoode and heard *1655*

25–27 (considering . . . victuals)] considering . . . victuals
and other necessaries, *1655*

27 were] was *1635 1655*

p. 23   8 and] *1635*, & *1631*, an *1655*

11–12 themselues . . . together] themselves together *1655*

23 such] *om. 1655*

24 men children] men-children *1655*

31 Murther] murder *1635 1655*
practised,] practised *1655*

p. 24   1 cause,] cause *1655*

5 God,] *1635*, God *1655*, *Dieties* [sic] (*MS addition*) *1631*

p. 25   7–8 after sayd] after said *1635*, *om. 1655*

p. 26   1 accomplish:] *1635 1655*, accomplish *1631*

6 grac'd] *1635 1655*, grac d *1631*

28 time: the] *1635 1655*, time. the *1631*

p. 27   18 so] *om. 1655*

21 Child,] *1635 1655*, Child. *1631*
waxe] waxt *1635*, waxed *1655*

23 discoursed of at large] *1655*, discoursed of large, *1631*,
discoursed of at lage *1635*

29–30 (that haue no rest)] (that he and the rest) *1635*,
parens. om. 1655

p. 28   3 no] not *1655*

11 but] *1635 1655*, bu *1631*

19 (as yet vnborne)] *parens. om. 1655*
24 ioy!] ioy? *1655*
26 will it] it will *1655*
29 my] thy *1655*
lie] will lie *1655*
32 doest] dost *1635,* do'st *1655*
33 (what … not)] *parens. om. 1655*

p. 29   7 in] of *1655*
8 (to … Story)] *parens. om. 1655*
9 a] on *1655*
13 Land.] Land: *1655*
18 Knights,] Knights *1655*
21–22 desire,] desire; *1635*

p. 30   7 a Ship-boord] on Ship-boord *1655*

p. 31   21 burnisht] the burnished *1655*
22 were] was *1655*
27 now] not *1655*

p. 32   9 beames] means *1655*
33 to] in *1655*

p. 33   8–9 her Chamber] the Chamber *1655*
16 made a] madés *1655*
21 his] *om. 1655*

p. 34   3 rid] *om. 1655*
10–11 vntimely] *1635 1655,* vntimelesse *1631*
20 her] this *1655*
21–22 (and … Queene)] *parens. om. 1655*
26 death.] *1635 1655,* death *1631*
34 Doctor,] Doctor *1635 1655*

p. 35   6 misfortune.] *1635 1655,* misfortune, *1631*
15 die.] *1635 1655,* die, *1631*

108

III

1–2 for shee had intitled him, The] she indeuored to
                   brand him with ignominy, for she had entitled him,
                   the *1655*
        4 assuredly] surely *1635 1655*
       10 as] *Ed., om. 1631 1635 1655*
       17 griefes] griefe *1635*, grief *1655*
       18 sounde] swoon *1655*
       21 sweat] *1655*, swate *1631 1635* (*see explanatory note*)
       29 a] *om. 1655*
       31 neuer] ever *1655*

1 wealth] wealth and treasure *1655*
       12 her] *om. 1655*
          Pyramus] *1635 1655*, Pryamus *1631*
       13 cruell] cruell and tyrranous *1655*
       20 hatefull] loathesome and hateful *1655*
       28 went] tooke his journey *1655*
       31 the Sea] Sea *1655*

1 CHAPTER 3] CHAP. VII *1635*, CHAP. III. *1655*
    13–14 Chamber, how] Chamber, which she kept exceeding clean
                   and handsome, how *1655*
       14 first] first of all *1655*
          then] then afterwards *1655*
       15 meetings] meeting *1655*
          wanton] amorous and wanton *1655*
    25–26 Virginities losse] virginities loue *1655*
       26 in] and in *1635 1655*

5 these] their *1655*
       15 seauen] some *1655*
       19 (whereinto he had led her)] *Ed.*, (whereinto ... her,
          1631 1635, ,whereinto ... her, *1655*

9 tempted] tempting *1655*
       10 as] as that *1655*
       12 with] with a *1655*

14 feede] *Ed.*, feeds *1631 1635*, feed *1655*
17 fiftly] *1635*, fitly *1631*, fifthly *1655*
18 seuenthly] *so in 1631 1635 1655* ("*sixthly*" *is omitted*)
21 my] *om. 1655*

p. 69   5 Lady] *om. 1655*
12 Tygers heart] tiger-heart *1655*
13 death.] *Ed.*, death, *1631*, death; *1635*, death: *1655*
14 the] *om. 1655*
17 to] in *1635 1655*
18 at] of *1655*
    gentle] gently *1655*
26 spilt, shall bee] it shall be *1655*
28 and the] *1635 1655*, and *1631*
29 Pooles] Poles *1655*

p. 70   15 riding] sliding *1635 1655* (*see note*)
    selfe] *1635 1655*, sefle *1631*
25 happen] happen'd *1655*

p. 71   7 see to] *1631 1635 1655* (*the second* to *may be a printer's addition*)
12 where] *1635 1655*, were *1631*
19 was] were *1655*

p. 72   2 said wales] same walls *1635 1655*
9–10 Their ... milke] Their of Almonds mixed with Goates milk, bread was made *1655*
14 aduentures,] *1655*, adventures *1631 1635*

p. 73   4 Castle,] Castle *1655*
8 Tarquinius,] Tarquinius *1655*
15 till] untill *1655*
16 Knight] *1655*, Knight, *1631 1635*
23 man; his steps] man his steps; *1655*
26 night] nihht *1655*

113

p. 74   12 habiliments] abiliments *1655*
              15 accidents;] accidents: *1655*
              29 Knight,] Knight *1655*
              30 hands. Day] hands; day *1655*
                 trauailed] travelled *1655*

p. 75   9–10 sea side] Sea-side *1655*
              17 Negars] Negers *1655*
              18 drowning] drowing *1655*
              29 farre] fare *1655*
              32 thy] my *1655*

p. 76   3 others] other *1635 1655*
               4 haue] hath *1655*
               7 neuer] neither *1655*
               9 hand, hee] *1655*, hand. Hee *1631 1635*
              12 heart-killing] heart killing and wofull *1655*
              16 therefore] *1635 1655*, there *1631*
              17 a periured] *1635 1655*, periured *1631*
              20 chaunces,] *1635 1655*, chaunces; *1631*

p. 77   1 this his] his *1655*
               8 from her] *1635 1655*, former *1631*
              10 foule.] *1635 1655*, foule, *1631*
              12 Knight,] *1635 1655*, Knight) *1631*
              17 knowledge] *1635 1655*, acknowledge *1631*
              30 thee] *1631*, the *1635 1655*

p. 78   8 assistants] *1635 1655*, assistance *1631*
              10 crueltie,] *Ed.*, crueltie; *1631*, cruelty, *1635 1655*
              15 things neuer] things that had *1655*
              19 Palmers] Pilgrims *1655*
              25 Palmer] Pilgrim *1655*

p. 79   3 man,] *1635 1655*, man? *1631*
              10 done] *om. 1655*
              11 chaunced] *1635 1655*, chaunched *1631*

13 bred] *1635 1655*, breed *1631*

16 Wildernesse.] *1635 1655*, Wildernesse, *1631*

21 about] *1635 1655*, aboue *1631*

p. 80   18 Sonne)] *1635 1655*, Sonne *1631*

19 (as did the blood of Abell)] *1635 1655*, *blacked out in 1631*

21 it. By] *1635 1655*, it, By *1631*

25 Reuenge:] *1635 1655*, Revenge, *1631*

25–26 Adulterie, defamed] *1635 1655*, Adulterie defamed *1631*

27 liues blood] lifes blood *1635 1655*

p. 81   2 voyce, saying] *1635 1655*, voyce saying *1631*

11 thy] *1655*, the *1631 1635*

p. 82   7 time (as] *1655*, (time as *1631 1635*

14 Armes.] *1655*, Armes, *1631 1635*

15 sight! This] *Ed.*, sight, This *1631 1635*, sight!
(quoth the Blacke Knight) This *1655*

26 drawne,] *1655*, drawne; *1631 1635*

31 (quoth ... Knight)] *1655*, quoth the (Blacke *1631 1635*

p. 83   1 burying] *1655*, buring *1631 1635*

2 agreed,] *1635 1655*, agreed *1631*

5 (which] *1635*, which *1631*, , which *1655*

9 lullababyes] lullabies *1635 1655*

9–10 rocked thee] *1635 1655*, rocked *1631*

12 beggeth] *Ed.*, begging *1631 1635 1655*

20 cruellnesse] crueltie *1635 1655*

22 intreaties] *1635 1655*, intreates *1631*

24 thee;] *1635*, thee, *1631 1655*

p. 84   7 Mother.] *1635*, Mother *1631*, mother. *1655*

9 threaten] *1655*, threatens *1631 1635*

19 with eyes sparkling] *1635 1655*, with spartling *1631*

27 blood.] *1635*, blood *1631*, blood: : *1655*

115

p. 85   19 this Knight] his Knight *1635*

34 which as then] which was then *1655*

p. 86   21 poyson,] poyson *1655*

pawes] pawe *1655*

feet] *Ed.*, foot *1631 1635 1655*

23 nor] no *1635 1655*

25 horrible] terrible *1655*

28 harmelesse] harmely *1655*

p. 87   18 of] off *1655*

this] the *1655*

22 beare] bare *1655*

30 a] *om. 1635 1655*

32 Heauens] heaven *1655*

p. 88   1 to] vnto *1655*

3 vnto] to *1655*

6 heare … see] see … hear *1655*

11 beset so thicke] so thick beset *1655*

12 shaddowy] *1655*, shaddow *1631 1635*

nor no Starre] nor Star *1655*

13 whereas] where *1655*

voyce] voyse *1655*

14 balefull] dolefull *1655*

18 flinty] flinted *1655*

20 shall serue] *1655*, shall, serue *1631 1635*

22 will] *1635 1655*, wil *1631* (*at end of line, probably for justification*)

24 whereas] where *1655*

28 new] *om. 1655*

30 distressed] greatly distressed *1655*

p. 89   5 of] in *1655*

8 of] in *1655*

9 for] *om. 1655*

were] *1655*, was *1631 1635*

11 cause,] *Ed.*, cause *1631 1635*, cause whereof was to
    find *1655*
14 onely] and will only *1655*
19 venerall] venereal *1655*
25 more heauier] *1631 1635*, more heavie *1655*
25–26 so cruelly] cruelly so *1655*
27 speake] speake in *1655*

    2 tasted,] tastes thereof, *1635 1655*
    3 sodainely] presently *1655*
    6 which] whom *1655*
    7 as] as if *1655*
10 faythes] faith *1655*
19 Heauen] Heavens *1655*
21 As] Or *1655*
22 hath] *Ed.*, haue *1631 1635 1655*
27 Epitaph] *1635 1655*, Epitaph) *1631*
28 death: onely] death: but *1655*
30 worthy] *om. 1655*

    4 way:] *Ed.*, way; *1631 1635*, way. *1655*
11 Court.] *1635 1655*, Court, *1631*
15 and] *1655*, an *1631 1635*
23–24 (which were very long)] *Ed.*, which were very long)
    1631 1635, , which were very long, *1655*
28 body;] *Ed.*, body, *1631 1635 1655*
29 diuided from his body] *1655*, diuided. *1631 1635*
33 reft] bereft *1655*

    2 confused] confounded *1655*
    9 halfe] false *1655*
14 with] on *1635*, in *1655*
15 and happy] *om. 1655*
18 meane] means *1655*
19 of] of my *1655*
21 Armes] arme *1655*
26 receiued] recouered *1635 1655*

29 on] vpon *1635 1655*
31 merily floting] and they merrily floated *1655*

p. 93

1 lippes they] lippes *1655*
17 builded vp] *om. 1655*
21 thinke] thinke it *1655*
   stayed they] they stayed *1635 1655*
26 these] the *1635*, they *1655*
29 in] in a *1655*
31 Marquesses] *om. 1655*
34 by a generall consent] *om. 1655*

p. 94

5 showne] done *1655*
   excepting] except *1655*
7 to] *om. 1655*
8 builded] built *1655*
15 which likewise was] with like solemnities *1655*
16 other Cities] *om. 1655*
   hath] was *1655*
18 Lincolne was, London is] Lincon [sic] is, London
   was *1655*

at $10 for all series. Prices for each series are based upon cost of printing and publication. Beginning in 1978, with the publication of Series IV, members will be billed $15 annual dues (student members, $10) regardless of whether there is a volume published during the year; all subscriptions will be used for printing and publishing costs, and members will be credited with the amount they have paid toward each series when it appears. Institutional members will be billed at time of publication.

Subscriptions should be sent to James M. Wells at The Newberry Library, 60 West Walton Street, Chicago, Illinois 60610. Institutional members are requested to provide, at the time of enrollment, any order numbers or other information required for their billing records; the Society cannot provide multiple invoices or other complex forms for their needs. Non-members may buy copies, at higher rates, of past publications as follows: Volume I, from Mr. Wells; Volumes II, III, and IV from the University of Chicago Press, 5801 Ellis Avenue, Chicago, Illinois 60637; and of Volumes V–VI and VII–VIII from the University of South Carolina Press, Columbia, South Carolina 29208.

FIRST SERIES

Vol. I. *Merie Tales of the Mad Men of Gotam*, by A. B., edited by Stanley J. Kahrl, and *The History of Tom Thumbe*, by R. I., edited by Curt F. Bühler, 1965.

Vol. II. Thomas Watson's Latin *Amyntas*, edited by Walter F. Staton, Jr., and Abraham Fraunce's translation, *The Lamentations of Amyntas*, edited by Franklin M. Dickey, 1967.

SECOND SERIES

Vol. III. *The Dyaloge Called Funus*, a translation of Erasmus's colloquy (1534), and *A Very Pleasant and Fruitful Diologe called The Epicure*, Gerrard's translation of Erasmus's colloquy (1545), edited by Robert R. Allen, 1969.

Vol. IV. *Leicester's Ghost*, by Thomas Rogers, edited by Franklin B. Williams, Jr., 1972.

THIRD SERIES

Vol. V–VI. *A Collection of Emblemes, Ancient and Moderne,* by George Wither, with introduction by Rosemary Freeman and bibliographical notes by Charles S. Hensley, 1975.

FOURTH SERIES

Vol. VII–VIII. *Tom a Lincolne,* by R. I., edited by Richard S. M. Hirsch, 1978.